BEACON STREET GIRLS

This book belongs to:

VERITAS AMICITIA GAUDIUM
truth friendship fun!

BEACON STREET GIRLS

Be sure to read all of our books:

BOOK 1 - worst enemies/best friends

BOOK 2 - bad news/good news

BOOK 3 - letters from the heart

BOOK 4 - out of bounds

BOOK 5 - promises, promises

BOOK 6 - lake rescue

BOOK 7 - freaked out

BOOK 8 - lucky charm

BOOK 9 - fashion frenzy

BOOK 10 - just kidding

BOOK 11 - ghost town

BOOK 12 - time's up

BOOK 13 - green algae and bubble gum wars

BOOK 14 - crush alert

BOOK 15 - the great scavenger hunt

BSG Special Adventure Books:

charlotte in paris

maeve on the red carpet

freestyle with avery

katani's jamaican holiday

isabel's texas two-step

Coming soon:

BSG SPECIAL ADVENTURE - ready! set! hawaii!

BOOK 16 - sweet thirteen

BEACON STREET GIRLS

Ghost Town

BY
ANNIE BRYANT

ALADDIN MIX

NEW YORK   LONDON   TORONTO   SYDNEY

Special thanks to Big Sky Resort for allowing us to use its name and location
as a fictional setting in this book.

ALADDIN MIX
An imprint of Simon & Schuster Children's Publishing Division
1230 Avenue of the Americas, New York, NY 10020
First Aladdin M!X edition September 2009
Text copyright © 2007 by B*tween Productions, Inc.,
Home of the Beacon Street Girls.

For information about special discounts for bulk purchases, please contact Simon & Schuster
Special Sales at 1-866-506-1949 or business@simonandschuster.com.
The Simon & Schuster Speakers Bureau can bring authors to your live event. For more
information or to book an event contact the Simon & Schuster Speakers Bureau
at 1-866-248-3049 or visit our website at www.simonspeakers.com.
Designed by Dina Barsky
The text of this book was set in Palatino Lynotype.
Manufactured in the United States of America
2 4 6 8 10 9 7 5 3 1
Library of Congress Control Number 2009921937
ISBN 978-1-4169-6441-4
ISBN 978-1-4169-9654-5 (eBook)

Who's Who

Katani Summers
aka Kgirl . . . Katani has a strong fashion sense and business savvy. She is stylish, loyal & cool.

Avery Madden
Avery is passionate about all sports and animal rights. She is energetic, optimistic & outspoken.

Charlotte Ramsey
A self-acknowledged "klutz" and an aspiring writer, Charlotte is all too familiar with being the new kid in town. She is intelligent, worldly & curious.

Isabel Martinez
Her ambition is to be an artist. She was the last to join the Beacon Street Girls. She is artistic, sensitive & kind.

Maeve Kaplan-Taylor
Maeve wants to be a movie star. Bubbly and upbeat, she wears her heart on her sleeve. She is entertaining, friendly & fun.

Ms. Razzberry Pink
The stylishly pink proprietor of the Think Pink boutique is chic, gracious & charming.

Marty
The adopted best dog friend of the Beacon Street Girls is feisty, cuddly & suave.

Happy Lucky Thingy and alter ego Mad Nasty Thingy
Marty's favorite chew toy, it is known to reveal its alter ego when shaken too roughly. He is most often happy.

more on beaconstreetgirls.com

Part One
Eureka!

1

The Secret's Out

After pouring the beans from the saucepan and grabbing the Tabasco sauce, Charlotte scanned the kitchen. She and her father had everything staged and ready to go. Now all they were missing were the guests. She scurried down the mammoth staircase to the foyer to wait. The giant grandfather clock on the landing seemed to be tick-tocking in slow motion.

Suddenly, Charlotte heard car doors and voices. "They're here!" she shouted to her father as she raced to pull open the front door before Maeve even had a chance to ring the bell.

"Charlotte! You scared me!" Maeve exclaimed, her hand instinctively going to her heart.

"Maeve! Mr. Taylor! You're here!" Charlotte cried, ushering them inside.

"Are we late? The invitation said eleven, right?" Mr. Taylor asked, taken aback by Charlotte's urgency.

"Yup! Eleven. Right on the button. Come on in. I'll take

your coats," Charlotte said excitedly, helping Mr. Taylor out of his black overcoat.

"Look at my hair!" Maeve moaned as she pulled down her hood. "Frizz City! I wish it was snow; rain just ruins my hair."

As soon as she'd hung their coats in the foyer, Charlotte spotted Isabel coming up the walk with her Aunt Lourdes. "Go ahead upstairs," Charlotte motioned to Maeve and Mr. Taylor. "My dad has some really delicious breakfast burritos ready."

"Isabel! Ms. Ortiz," Charlotte said, opening the door while they were still on the porch steps.

"Oh, please, Charlotte, you know you girls can call me Aunt Lourdes. I'm sorry, but Isabel's mother couldn't make it this morning. She sends her best. I know the invitation said you wanted parents to attend. I hope it is all right that I have come instead."

"Of course. Of course!" Charlotte eagerly welcomed Isabel and her aunt into the cavernous foyer. "Here, let me take your coats." Suddenly, the doorbell rang again.

Immediately, Marty let out a howl from somewhere upstairs. The doorbell always sent the BSG's little terrier mix into a frenzy. He came flying downstairs, convinced that anyone who came to the door was there to see him. Marty spun around in excited circles, jumping at the door.

"Just a minute," Charlotte sang out, trying to pull Marty back, afraid she might bonk him as she opened the big door.

"MARTY!" Avery shouted when Charlotte opened the

door. Her rain jacket sprayed droplets in every direction as she rolled around on the floor, wrestling with her favorite pooch.

"Good morning, Charlotte. What a lively party," Mrs. Madden laughed as she and Charlotte stared at the scene in front of them.

"Where's Happy Lucky Thingy? Let's get it!" Avery shouted as she and Marty rocketed past them up the stairs.

"Charlotte!" Maeve suddenly reappeared at Charlotte's side, grabbing her friend's arm and pulling her upstairs to the table in the dining room. "Denim place mats and bandanna napkins! And the place cards! Über cute. You did this? And you spelled our names out with little pieces of rope?"

"It's really only twine, but it looks like rope, doesn't it?" Charlotte was proud of her handiwork.

"So cute! But what does it all mean? Come on, Char, spill it! What IS the special occasion?" Maeve asked, lowering her voice to a conspiring whisper.

Charlotte opened her mouth, but the doorbell rang again and she had a good excuse to break away.

"Gotta get the door, Maeve. You'll find out soon. SOON!" Charlotte breathed a sigh of relief. *That was close!*

Katani was waiting at the door with both parents. "Hello everyone," Charlotte greeted Mr. and Mrs. Summers and her friend. "Come on in."

At last, Charlotte thought as she pranced up the stairs behind the three Summerses. *All the BSG are here. We can sit down, eat . . . and TELL.*

Unfortunately, Mr. Ramsey was busy talking to Mr. Taylor about the weather. *The weather! Who cares about the weather?* Charlotte thought as she sat down. She glanced at Isabel across the table and shook her head impatiently.

"Dad," Charlotte complained as she nudged him under the table.

"You don't want me to wait until we're finished eating?" Mr. Ramsey asked with a grin.

"DAD!" Charlotte gave her father a look that meant *enough, already!*

"Okay," he said to Charlotte, squeezing her hand as he tapped on his juice glass to get everyone's attention.

"You all are probably wondering why Charlotte and I asked you here this morning," Mr. Ramsey said affably. "Well, as you know, I'm a travel writer. Books mainly, but I do fill in here and there with freelance work for travel magazines." Mr. Ramsey paused to take a sip of coffee and Charlotte looked around the table.

"*International Travel,* a magazine that I've written for before, would like me to do a piece on a resort in Montana," Mr. Ramsey continued.

Maeve was still admiring the decorations, but Charlotte could see that an idea was clicking in her head. Charlotte nudged her dad again. She wanted him to get to the point.

Mr. Ramsey winked at her and went on. "My daughter is getting impatient, so here it is, folks. Big Sky Resort wants to attract families, so they invited me to write an article about their activities for older kids and teenagers. I explained that I only had one daughter, but if I could bring her friends, I could really get an idea of what the experience would be like."

On the word *friends*, Maeve sucked in a huge breath. Her eyes latched onto Charlotte's. "Does this mean what I think it does?" Maeve gasped.

Charlotte gave all her friends a megawatt smile.

"So that's why I invited you all here today," Mr. Ramsey announced. "I am hoping that all of you will give me your permission to take the girls on a little Beacon Street Girls adventure—so to speak—to Big Sky Resort in Montana."

"O-o-o-o-oh, ho-o-o-o-ome, home on the range," Maeve crooned. The whole table giggled. Always the performer, Maeve *would* be the one to burst into song.

Marty seemed to know this song too, because he began to yowl along in perfect harmony.

Even Avery stopped mid-bite. That said something. Athletic Avery was famous for her appetite. "Seriously? A trip? All of us together? *Yippppeee-ki-ayyyy*! So it's like a dude ranch, right? That means horses and skiing and snowboarding and snowmobiling and—"

Katani grabbed onto Charlotte's wrist. "You knew this all along, didn't you! I can't believe you didn't tell us!"

"It was so hard to keep quiet," Charlotte confessed, relieved at last that the secret was out. And what a commotion it was causing!

Everyone started talking at once. Avery's shouts of "Yippee-ki-ay!" mingled with Maeve and Marty's unique version of "Home on the Range" as the parents at the table discussed the specifics of the trip.

Charlotte beamed as she looked around at the happy gathering. It hadn't been easy keeping quiet about such a big secret, but this moment was totally worth it. She couldn't wait to fill in her friends on all the incredible details!

CHAPTER

2

Details! Details!

s the BSG brunch bunch chatted excitedly and Marty spun around in excitement, Charlotte's laughter caught in her throat when she saw that Isabel was staring down at her plate.

Maeve's father, Mr. Taylor, cleared his throat and caught Mr. Ramsey's eye. "Richard, I think this trip is a wonderful opportunity, but I have to ask . . . is it going to be expensive? Because I'm not sure . . ."

As Maeve's dad trailed off, Mr. Ramsey nodded his head and held up his hand. "The magazine has offered to foot the whole bill." Mr. Ramsey used his knife to clink on his juice glass. Eager eyes rested on Charlotte's dad. "The only thing the girls will need to bring is some spending money . . . I'd say that two hundred dollars should be sufficient. And, of course, no one can go without her parents' permission."

"Well, that sounds quite reasonable," Mrs. Madden said with a wide smile. "I say go for it!"

Avery let out a huge cheer and gave her mother a gigantic hug. "Ooof. Easy, Avery. You can use some of your savings from your dog walking business," Mrs. Madden pointed out as she hugged her super-excited daughter.

Charlotte giggled as Avery and Marty exchanged paw-fives. Luckily, Charlotte had been saving money for several months too. She'd been helping her landlady, Miss Pierce, with astronomy research on the Internet and by running errands. Charlotte was relieved she'd be able to take $200 out of her savings and not drain the whole account on this trip.

"Does anyone have questions?" Mr. Ramsey asked.

"I do, Mr. Ramsey," Aunt Lourdes said, looking very serious and stern. Isabel glanced at her aunt nervously. Mrs. Martinez's sister was a kind woman, but she was also very strict, and often embarrassed Isabel with her never-ending questions.

"Certainly." Mr. Ramsey turned his attention toward Isabel's aunt.

Aunt Lourdes leaned forward, pursed her lips, and narrowed her eyes. "Will there be any *other* chaperones on the trip?"

"Noooo, just me." Mr. Ramsey seemed a bit taken aback by Aunt Lourdes' intensity. "But I've led travel expeditions in the Serengeti with groups of twenty people . . . so five girls shouldn't be a problem," Mr. Ramsey assured Isabel's skeptical aunt.

Charlotte bit her lip. She had been crossing her fingers that Isabel's aunt wouldn't react this way to the news.

The room, which had been ringing with laughter just moments before, was now completely silent.

Charlotte stole a glance at Isabel, whose pink cheeks said it all. Charlotte couldn't see Isabel's eyes, but it was clear that her friend was embarrassed beyond belief!

Mr. Ramsey smiled at Aunt Lourdes and politely nodded his head. "I can see why you might be concerned. I'm sure I would have questions if I were sending Charlotte away, too. Let me assure you, Lourdes. Let me assure all of you," Mr. Ramsey said, looking around the table at all the parents gathered there. "This is a fact-finding trip. I will have people to talk to while I'm there, but mostly my job at Big Sky Resort is to see how kids in this age group—our kids—enjoy the facility. I will be spending my time with the girls. I won't be involved in writing the article until I return to Boston."

Finally, Aunt Lourdes broke into a smile. "Well . . . I suppose that could be all right."

Charlotte popped out of her chair and began gathering dirty dishes from the table. As she passed Isabel, Charlotte casually asked, "Want to give me a hand in the kitchen, Izzy?"

Isabel nodded and stood up, quickly stacking plates in front of her. She didn't say a word as she followed Charlotte into the kitchen, where she began rinsing off the dishes in the sink and handing them to Charlotte to arrange in the dishwasher.

"Are you okay, Isabel?" Charlotte asked as she took a plate and flicked a small piece of burrito into the disposal.

Isabel squeezed her eyes shut and shook her head.

"Is it Aunt Lourdes?"

Isabel nodded slowly and shrugged her shoulders.

"Iz, we all know how protective your aunt is. You don't

have to be embarrassed about *anything* around us.

"It's not that . . . well, not *only* that." Isabel turned on the water again and started rinsing off salsa-covered forks and knives.

"You don't think your Aunt Lourdes will convince your mother that the trip is a bad idea—" Charlotte stopped short. The possibility took her breath away. This was supposed to be the trip of a lifetime with *all* her best friends. Three out of four just wouldn't do.

Isabel turned off the water and gazed out the window.

Charlotte closed the dishwasher and leaned against the counter. "Isabel? What's wrong? You can tell me . . . whatever it is." She waited in silence for Isabel to speak.

"It's not just Aunt Lourdes," Isabel repeated, her eyes misting over.

There was a weird silence in the kitchen now that they weren't clattering dishes and silverware and the water was shut off. The two could hear Isabel's aunt asking "Will they wear helmets?" in a serious tone.

Isabel looked up at Charlotte and the two burst into a fit of giggles.

"Helmets?" Isabel threw her hands in the air. "What *will* she come up with next? Nutrition? PG-13 movies on the plane?"

Charlotte was glad to see Isabel joking around again. She was almost back to her usual cheerful self.

"But even if Aunt Lourdes gets all of her questions answered, and even if Mama gives me permission to go, I'm still not sure if . . ." Isabel hesitated. "Um, if . . ."

In the next room, Charlotte could hear her friends'

voices piping into the conversation. Maybe they had convinced Aunt Lourdes that everything would be all right.

"You're not sure if . . ." Charlotte prompted, trying to help Isabel finish her thought.

"I'm not sure if my family can afford it," Isabel murmured softly, looking down.

"The two hundred dollars?" Charlotte asked.

"Two hundred dollars is a lot of money for us," Isabel reacted defensively. "Besides," she added in a low voice, "sometimes I worry about my mom when I'm away."

Charlotte nodded, biting her lip. "I understand." Having lost her own mother at a young age, Charlotte could readily empathize with Isabel's concern about her mom, who was ill with multiple sclerosis. She reached over and gave her friend a hug. "Don't worry too much, Izzy. Your sister and your aunt will be with her. I'm sure she'll be okay."

"Oh, Char, you're right. But even if my mom is okay, the money thing is still a big deal for me. There's just not enough for extras right now. And two hundred dollars to go to a resort seems like a really big extra. I think—no, I KNOW—that it's just not possible." Isabel brushed a tear from her cheek.

"Hey, you two! What are you doing in there?" Maeve called from the other room. "Get out here!"

"What's going on?" Charlotte asked, hurrying back to the dining room. Isabel followed, discreetly wiping tears from her eyes.

"It's time to concentrate on OUR plans," Maeve announced. "The Beacon Street Girls are going to a real dude ranch!"

"I can't believe it! We're all going to Montana! To a dude ranch! YEEEE HAAAW!" Avery shouted. "Your dad said something about free lift tickets, right?" she asked. "That means skiing and snowboarding! I'll be able to practice my boarding so next time I visit Dad in Colorado, I'll be in top form!"

"Oh, I almost forgot. We sent away for brochures so you can read about everything." Charlotte raced for the stash of brochures stacked on her father's desk and passed one to each girl. Charlotte's heart sank as Isabel placed hers on the table without even looking at it.

The rest of the girls pored over the glossy pictures, gushing over every detail about the ranch and its amenities.

"Look at the rooms! They're so elegant and totally posh. Cowboy posh. I feel like a princess just looking at them!" Maeve swooned.

"Whoa, check out the game room. Pool tables and video games and air hockey. I rock at air hockey!" Avery pumped her fist in the air.

"It says here they offer horseback riding and have dozens of riding trails." Katani looked ecstatic. "I can't wait to try western-style riding! And the resort has sleigh rides with complimentary hot chocolate!"

"YEEEE HAWWW!" Avery shouted out again.

"*Ouch*," Katani said as she rubbed her ears. "Take it down a notch, Ave."

"Come on, guys, this calls for a group hug." Maeve pulled the BSG toward her, and the five melded together into one big BSG hug.

Isabel was to Charlotte's right, and Charlotte could

sense how tense she was. She gave Isabel an extra reassuring squeeze with her right arm. Somehow they had to make this work out. Their dream trip wouldn't be perfect unless Isabel was part of it.

The Great Compromise

As Maeve's brother played with Marcia and Jan (the names du jour of her adorable guinea pigs), Maeve hopped up and raced to the computer. She logged online and hoped that some of the BSG would be there to talk about their trip. Maeve clicked away at the keyboard.

"Maeve! MAEVE!" she heard her mother calling from the kitchen.

Maeve signed off, took a deep breath, and forced a bright smile. She'd heard that smiling could actually put you in a better mood.

"Maeve, Mom's calling," Sam told her.

"I know, I know. Take care of Marcia and Jan for me, okay?" she instructed as she opened the door.

Maeve was a little surprised to see her father still sitting in the kitchen. She hadn't known he was coming by today.

"Maeve," her dad began with a small smile, then stopped when he saw her downcast expression.

"What's the matter, sweetheart?" asked Ms. Kaplan, her face filled with concern.

"Isabel has no money for the trip and we just can't leave her behind. It would be so tragic for her," Maeve explained with a dramatic flourish. She slumped down in the kitchen chair and sighed.

"I think we might possibly have a solution," Mr. Taylor said with a wide grin. "Your mother and I were a little concerned about the money as well, but we will contribute half the money for your trip . . ."

"And you will have to earn the other half yourself," Ms. Kaplan added firmly.

Maeve looked at her parents and gulped. "I have to earn one hundred dollars?"

"If you want to go on the trip . . . yes," her dad confirmed with a nod.

"Before the trip or after the trip?"

"Before the trip, of course," Ms. Kaplan emphasized. "You can't spend money that you don't have."

"But it's only ten days away!" Maeve exclaimed. "How can I earn a hundred dollars in ten days? And how does that help Isabel?" she asked, searching her parents' faces for answers.

Ms. Kaplan's mouth curled into a smile. "Actually, your father and I have an idea."

Maeve looked over at her father.

"I was thinking of hosting a Western Movie Festival at the Movie House next weekend. Just because everyone seems to be in a western type of mood. What if you set up a little stand with refreshments for all the moviegoers? It would be a good experience for you to organize a menu, buy food within a budget, and serve the guests," Mr. Taylor said.

"Menu? Budget?" Maeve asked. She was an idea person, not an organizer!

"Well, you have to figure out the food costs and make a budget before you can sell anything," Ms. Kaplan pointed out.

"We have some money from season ticket sales that I'll lend you for purchasing the food and beverages. So, whatever profit you make after you subtract your expenses, you can keep," Mr. Taylor said with a smile.

"But, what about Isabel?" an anxious Maeve insisted. She just couldn't let her friend down. Her father stood up and gave Maeve a hug.

"Honey, I am so proud of you for thinking about your friend too. Why don't you girls do it together?"

Maeve smiled up at her dad as her head began spinning with visions of one hundred dollar bills. This might just work. "Thank you! THANK YOU!" she exclaimed, giving them both a hug and a kiss on the cheek before racing for her room.

"Don't go overboard and bite off more than you can chew," her mother called after her.

Maeve didn't have time to respond to or even think about her mother's comment. She *had* to call Isabel immediately and let her know that now maybe they could both earn the money for the trip. If they worked together, it would be a piece of cake. Hah, *literally*! Maeve thought with a giggle.

As she popped a Swedish Fish in her mouth, Maeve thought of her friend Ethel Weiss. Owner of Irving's Toy and Card Shop, where Maeve constantly restocked her supply of Swedish Fish, Ethel was a great businesswoman. *She'd be so proud of me*, Maeve thought happily.

They were *all* going to Big Sky Resort after all. It was just a matter of time and hard work and planning and good food. Maeve couldn't help letting out a squeal as she grabbed the phone.

3

Cowgirl Up!

Sunday night was Family Night at the Summers' house, and Family Night dinners were always scrumptious. Tonight it was roasted chicken, a huge, fresh chopped salad—Katani's personal favorite—with Patrice's balsamic vinaigrette, mashed potatoes and gravy, and spinach au gratin, topped off with Mrs. Fields' homemade sweet potato pudding.

"I have an announcement," Mr. Summers proclaimed as soon as they started passing dishes. "Katani has been offered the chance to visit a dude ranch in Montana."

"A dude ranch in Montana? The Wild Wild West?" Mrs. Fields marveled. "Sounds like a wonderful educational opportunity!" In addition to being Katani's grandmother, Mrs. Fields was also the principal of Abigail Adams Junior High School.

"Dude ranch? Dude ranch? Is that a place for cool dudes?" Kelley asked, drizzling dressing onto her salad. Katani's fifteen-year-old sister Kelley was autistic, which meant that she had trouble communicating and interacting with other people and often seemed much younger than her age.

"We have brochures for you to look at after supper," Katani told Kelley.

"Montana . . . Fontana. That sounds far away. How are you going to get to Montana?" Kelley asked.

"She'll fly in an airplane," Mrs. Summers said.

"NO WAY!" Patrice complained. "I can't believe that Katani is going to get to fly before I do! That's unfair."

"Mr. Ramsey is a travel writer and he's writing an article for a magazine about kids' experiences at this resort. He worked it out with the magazine so that Charlotte and her friends could go on this trip with him and be part of his research. The magazine is picking up expenses," Mrs. Summers explained.

"How long is she going to be gone?" Patrice asked as she furiously buttered a potato roll. Katani couldn't help but feel a tiny bit bad that her big sister seemed so envious.

"A week," Katani told her. Patrice and Katani often competed with each other, but this time Katani sympathized with Patrice. Missing out on a trip to a resort was huge.

"A week!" Patrice exclaimed, dropping her knife to her plate with a clunk. "My little sister gets to spend a week at a dude ranch while I'm stuck here? You know what that means! I'll be babysitting Kelley every single day!"

Kelley dropped her roll onto her plate and glared at Patrice. "Babysit! You do NOT babysit, Patrice! You

Kelley-sit," she said, sticking out her lower lip and crossing her arms in front of her.

"Sorry, Kelley," Patrice mumbled. "You're right, I Kelley-sit. And we have a lot of fun, right?" Sometimes it was hard to be patient with Kelley, but all of the Summers sisters tried their best to help Kelley out and be cheerful about it.

As Mr. and Mrs. Summers went on about the plans for the upcoming trip, Kelley pushed away from the table and returned with Mr. Bear, her favorite stuffed animal.

"Here, Katani," Kelley said, shoving Mr. Bear into Katani's lap. "Mr. Bear can stay with you so you're not sad." Suddenly, her voice changed and her lip quivered. "You don't have to go away. I don't want you to go away!"

"Katani's not sad." Mrs. Summers looked over at her daughter. "Are you?"

"You have been surprisingly quiet through all this," Mrs. Fields noted. "What's going on, Katani?" she asked her granddaughter.

"Well, I was excited about the trip, but . . ." Katani trailed off.

"You *do* want to go on this trip, don't you? Montana is a beautiful part of the country, and you'll get to experience life in the West with all your friends. It's really quite a wonderful opportunity," Mrs. Summers said.

"It's not that I don't want to go. It sounds amazing. It's just that . . ."

"Are you afraid to fly?" Patrice asked.

"No! Not at all. It's just . . ."

"Mr. Bear can go with you if you are afraid to be away from home," Kelley comforted her.

"Thanks, Kelley, but it's not about being homesick or anything. It's the whole two hundred dollars thing," Katani finally admitted.

"But I thought the magazine was paying for everything," Patrice said.

"Mr. Ramsey said that the girls should bring two hundred dollars for spending money," Mr. Summers said. "Katani, you have more than enough in your savings account to cover that."

"I know. I know. But I'm not sure that I want to dig into my savings for this trip," Katani explained.

There was complete silence around the table. The family was too dumbfounded to respond.

Patrice folded her arms and started to smirk. "Are you serious, Katani?"

Katani rolled her eyes. "What? I've worked hard to earn that money! I've been selling my scarves for a couple of months now and I've been saving that money for the future . . . here, let me show you." Katani got up from the table and came back with her business notebook. There were the figures, in black and white. "See, if I put money into my savings account every month and then the money gathers interest, I'll have just enough money to launch my design business by the time I turn twenty-one." Katani was determined to be a big-time international designer with her own Kgirl Fashion Empire someday. Taking out two hundred dollars now would only set her back from her goals.

"An international design business? When you're twenty-one?" Patrice scoffed.

Katani said nothing in response. She felt her cheeks grow warm and crossed her arms in front of her to keep her hands from shaking. Patrice could make her so mad sometimes.

"Now, Patrice. You should respect Katani's ambitions," Mrs. Fields chided. "Have you ever heard the story of the ant and the grasshopper? The ant works and toils and saves up his food and lives comfortably through the winter. The grasshopper spends all his time chirping and singing and when the winter comes, he has no food saved. Katani is right to think carefully about how to spend her money."

"Katani, perhaps we can finish this discussion after dinner in the living room," Mr. Summers suggested.

"Meaning, I'm not going on a dream vacation *and* I'll have to do the dishes, too," Patrice grumbled. "Unfair."

"I believe it was your turn to do the dishes anyway." Mrs. Summers flashed her stern lawyer look at Patrice, who clamped her mouth shut and moved some spinach around her plate with her fork. Nobody talked back to Mrs. Summers.

After the dishes were cleared, Katani and her parents moved to the living room.

"Your father and I appreciate that you have respect for money and that you work hard and save so carefully," Mrs. Summers began.

"It's very admirable that you have such lofty goals," Mr. Summers added. "Especially for someone your age."

"But this is a once-in-a-lifetime experience," Mrs. Summers continued. "You've worked very hard in school this year. Don't you think you deserve a nice vacation?"

Katani hadn't been thinking about it that way.

"I don't want to intrude, but I thought I could offer some help." Mrs. Fields poked her head into the living room.

"Of course, Mom, come on in." Mrs. Summers motioned Mrs. Fields into the room.

Mrs. Fields dug fifty dollars out of her purse and handed it to her granddaughter.

"Grandma Ruby, no . . . no, thank you. I don't want to take any money from you or Mom and Dad," Katani said, gently pushing her grandmother's hand back.

"Katani, I am your grandmother. I want to give this money to you. It's an investment," Mrs. Fields said firmly.

"What?" Katani looked puzzled.

"An investment in your future. I'm banking on my money having great returns," Mrs. Fields said with a smile.

"I don't understand."

"Travel is broadening. It's inspiring. It's as necessary for a young up-and-coming designer as money in a savings account," Mrs. Fields told her.

Katani blushed. It felt good to know that her grandmother believed in her.

"You are going to come back from this experience rejuvenated. They call Montana Big Sky Country, you know. You'll get inspiration from that big sky and the beautiful rolling hills. And the people! The people you'll meet there will be different from folks in Boston."

"Really? What will they be like?" Katani asked.

"I'll be waiting for you to tell me all about them." Mrs. Fields smiled.

Katani couldn't help but smile right back.

"All work and no play makes Katani a dull designer, to put my own twist on an old phrase. Your designs should reflect a life full of wonder and adventure. This is an amazing opportunity for you, Katani. *Carpe diem*—seize the day!"

"Besides," Mr. Summers added. "You're twelve! You're supposed to have fun when you're twelve! There's plenty of time later for you to worry about finances."

"Like when you have your own daughters in college," Mrs. Summers added with a laugh.

Kelley came into the room, holding out Mr. Bear to her sister again. "Hey, Katani, Mr. Bear wants to visit the dude ranch with you."

Katani wasn't sure how Kelley sometimes knew just the right thing to say. She often thought Kelley understood what was going on better than most people.

"So, what do you say? Are you going to Montana?" Mrs. Fields asked.

"Yup!" Katani announced. "I'm going to Montana!"

"Yay!" Kelley cheered. "When are you going?"

"During school vacation." Katani's eyes widened. "Whoa! That's less than two weeks away!"

"But Katani . . . my horse show is in two weeks!" Kelley cried out. "Katani, you can't go in two weeks. You can't miss the horse show! Wilbur will be so sad." Wilbur was the horse Kelley rode in the therapeutic riding program at the High Hopes Riding Stable.

Katani hadn't realized until that moment that the two events would overlap. She suddenly felt panicked all over again. How could she leave Kelley at a time like this? The show was being put together for all of the kids with disabilities at the stable, and Kelley had been looking forward to the whole family being there to see her ride. Plus, Katani had wanted to help out at the event.

"Don't worry. I'll be there, Kelley," Patrice said from the doorway. Katani wasn't sure how long Patrice had been standing there. "And I'll borrow my friend's video camera. We'll videotape the whole thing, and Katani can watch it when she gets back."

Kelley still looked a little skeptical.

"You'll see, Kelley. We'll all be there to cheer you on. I bet Candice will even come home from college," Patrice said, giving Kelley's hand a squeeze. "Katani will be sending you cheers, too . . . all the way from Montana!"

Kelley's grimace slowly turned into a grin. "Okay," she conceded, "but Katani, you have to watch my Wilbur video the *minute* you get back."

4

The Big Idea

Whoa! Maeve, slow down," Avery said between bites. "You lost me somewhere between Cary Grant and mucho spending money."

"Hey! You're the one who wanted me to hurry up!" Maeve protested. She checked her watch. Yikes! With all their different after-school activities, she was able to get only fifteen minutes with the BSG at Montoya's to brainstorm for the Western Movie Festival.

I guess that's just life when your friends are very busy and important, Maeve thought to herself with a smug smile.

"Maeve and Isabel need help raising the two hundred dollars for the trip," Katani explained matter-of-factly. "So we're all going to pitch in by setting up a food table at the Western Movie Festival this weekend."

"Oh! That does sound cool!" Avery motioned for Maeve to continue.

"As I was saying," Maeve said, taking a deep, dramatic

breath, "I thought we could have a real hoedown."

"A hoedown?" Isabel asked. "Isn't that, like, a square dance or something?"

"You know what I mean—a western theme. I loved the way Charlotte decorated her place for the brunch. Imagine the Movie House like that—bales of hay, red bandanas, cowboy hats. Ooh, I have this sequined cowgirl outfit from my dance class that'd be perfect!"

"Maeve, I'm not sure the decorations and costumes are what we should be worrying about right now," Katani started to say.

The girls exchanged looks as Maeve presented her to-do list with a grand "ta-dah!"

"Maeve, there are like twenty-five different things there," Charlotte exclaimed.

"I have an idea. Why don't we just stick to snack food?" Isabel suggested. "People love to grab quick snacks at the movies."

"But . . ." Maeve protested, afraid that her dream of a western hoedown feast was being swept away like popcorn on the Movie House floor.

"Maeve," Katani said, "the point here isn't to throw a huge party with gourmet food. It's to raise as much money as we can in a short amount of time. So I say we pick things that are cheap and that we can sell for a good profit. And we can all wear bandanas!"

Maeve looked at Katani like she was speaking Greek.

"Trust me, Maeve," Katani reasoned. "In this case, less is definitely more."

"Elena Maria makes a great homemade salsa. And

tortilla chips from warehouse stores are always super cheap," Isabel recommended.

"Great idea!" Avery agreed. "Your sister's salsa rocks!"

"And she also makes the best jalapeño cornbread," Isabel proudly assured them.

"Hey, I bet my brother would help us. He makes the most awesome cookies and cupcakes," Avery added.

"Your brother would really do that?" Maeve asked.

Avery nodded slyly. She knew Scott would be willing to help out if he heard Elena Maria was involved. Avery had heard him on the phone with his friend the other day talking about how cute Elena was.

Maeve was still disappointed that she wasn't going to serve ribs and corn on the cob. And even if they couldn't get bales of hay, she was going to wear her cowgirl outfit no matter what. "Okay, it's tutor time. I gotta run," Maeve announced, gathering her things and zipping her backpack. "Think of some ideas, okay? And thanks so much for your help, everybody. You guys are the best."

"How are we going to get this all together?" a practical Charlotte asked after Maeve left.

"Hey, we can use my house," Avery offered. "We have a huge kitchen! Besides, since Scott will be doing the baking, he'll probably want to use the oven he's used to," she said.

"Good. Okay, so here's what we've got." Katani read from the list. "Charlotte and I will make flyers and pass them out at school and all around the neighborhood. The first step is to get people to come to the festival so they'll buy all this food. We will also be in charge of making the world's yummiest lemonade."

"Scott and Elena Maria could pass out flyers at the high school, too," Avery suggested.

"Perfect!" Katani made a note. "Avery and Scott will do the grocery shopping before Thursday night."

Avery nodded. "Elena should probably come, too," she added.

"And we'll all meet at Avery's on Thursday to bake and get everything organized," Katani finished, putting the list back on the table.

Isabel looked around at her friends and added, "Thanks, you guys. I really hope this works."

"It's *going* to work," Katani promised. "It has to."

No (Apron) Strings Attached

"They live *here*?" Elena Maria gaped as the group rang the bell at Avery's enormous colonial house on Warren Street.

Isabel had been there many times, but she hadn't forgotten the first time she saw the Maddens' house. She knew exactly what her sister was feeling. If Elena thought the outside was impressive, wait until she saw the inside.

"*Buenas noches*," Carla, the Madden's housekeeper, greeted the girls at the door. "All the BSG are in the kitchen."

"*Buenas noches*, Carla . . . *gracias*," Isabel replied with a friendly smile.

"Oh, *wow*," Elena Maria exclaimed, looking around the huge foyer with its gleaming black-and-white tile floor, circular staircase, and dazzling chandelier. "I've only seen stuff like this on TV!"

"Wait till you see the kitchen," Isabel whispered.

"There you are!" Avery called as Isabel and Elena Maria came through the kitchen door.

Isabel heard Elena Maria stifle a gasp. The kitchen looked like something right from the Food Channel. All the latest cooking gadgets were lined up on the marble counters. It was every chef's dream kitchen.

"Hey," Scott said, turning around and waving right at Elena Maria. Elena gave him a shy smile as she admired the gigantic kitchen.

"Here. Put these on." Avery handed each of the BSG an apron, while the girls stared back with dropped jaws. "What?! Just because I don't care about dirty clothes doesn't mean I don't believe in aprons!"

Charlotte and Katani, who had been unpacking bags of lemons, tied on their aprons and started juicing for the lemonade. Meanwhile, Maeve organized the other groceries into piles on the counter.

"Here, let me tie the back for you," Scott offered gallantly as Elena Maria struggled to get her apron on.

Isabel and Avery exchanged knowing glances.

"I can't wait to try your famous salsa," Scott said as he carefully tied the strings of Elena Maria's apron.

Isabel observed her sister as she eyed the bowls, the ceramic stove top, and the huge stainless steel side-by-side freezer and refrigerator. "This looks like the set of a cooking show," Elena Maria commented.

Scott laughed a little too enthusiastically. "I wish! How

cool would that be? I'd love to have my own show some-day. I'd call it *Scorching with Scott*."

"Scorching?" Elena Maria raised her eyebrows with a giggle, making Scott turn pink.

"Well, it's a working title." He chuckled.

Just then Mrs. Madden came through the back door with a stack of pizza boxes and set them on the table in the breakfast nook. "Pizza everyone!" she called out.

"Perfect timing, Mom. I'm starving!" Avery exclaimed as she bounced over to help her mom.

"I thought it was a good idea. I didn't want a kitchen full of hungry cooks eating up all the profits from your fundraiser!" Mrs. Madden said with a grin.

"I wish Aunt Lourdes had a kitchen like this." Elena Maria sighed as she took a bite of warm chicken-and-broccoli pizza.

"You can come cook in our kitchen anytime," Scott assured her quickly.

Now Elena Maria was the one to turn pink. She turned her back on the girls and quickly changed the subject. "So, um, how is this convection oven different from a regular oven?" Elena Maria asked Scott.

"Oh, let me show you." Scott ushered Elena Maria over to the ovens and away from the giggling girls in the breakfast nook.

When they finished their pizza, Isabel and Avery got to work chopping onions and garlic. "So, I'm dying to know the secret to your salsa," they overheard Scott saying to Elena Maria. The girls tried to listen to the conversation without making it obvious.

"Well, always use fresh tomatoes and fresh hot chili peppers, but the real secret ingredient is . . ." Elena Maria leaned close and whispered into Scott's ear. Avery nudged Isabel. Izzy, who disliked her sister's current boyfriend, Jimmy, intensely, crossed her fingers on both hands. It certainly seemed like things were heating up in the Madden kitchen, and it wasn't just Elena Maria's salsa!

Cookie Rush!

"Two cookies for fifty cents a piece? That'll be one dollar, please," Avery calculated, putting her hand out to a high school couple on their way into the movie theater.

"Guys, the movie is starting in two minutes," Maeve announced to some of their seventh-grade classmates, who were crowding around the treats at the table. "You better hurry . . . you don't want to miss the previews!"

"Can I have some more pink lemonade? This stuff rocks! What did you put in it?" Dillon asked.

Katani and Charlotte shared a look. They had used Grandma Ruby's lemonade recipe, which had been passed on from *her* grandmother. What they had put in it was strawberries, which sweetened the drink without overwhelming the natural lemon flavor.

"It's a family recipe . . . top secret," Katani smiled.

Avery was glad that so many kids from their class had shown up for the first show. Scott assured her that even more kids from the high school would be there for the second show.

"Come on, guys, you need to get in there," Maeve directed her classmates. "The movie is *starting*. I hate it when people come in late. It wrecks the whole mood of the thea-*tour*," Maeve complained dramatically.

"Chill out, Kaplan-Taylor. We're sitting in the balcony, so we won't wreck anything—I swear. You guys want to come too?" Billy Trentini asked the girls behind the table.

"We have a little cleaning up to do and then we have to set up for intermission and the second movie," Katani said. "But go on in. Enjoy the show." Kgirl was all business.

"One more cupcake for the road!" Riley Lee declared. He grabbed a chocolate cupcake and shoved a dollar bill in Avery's direction.

"As class president, I think I should get a free cupcake," piped in Henry Yurt, aka the Yurtmeister.

"Hmm, I guess so," Isabel said. She opened her sketchbook and quickly drew a picture of a Yurtbird with a cupcake in his beak. She ripped the piece of paper out and handed it to Henry. "Here you go!" she said. "A free cupcake for the president."

Henry held the drawing to his chest and pretended to swoon. "I will cherish it forever!" he promised.

Maeve leaned over and whispered to Isabel, "There goes our president—fearless leader and hopeless romantic!"

Isabel giggled and pushed back her long, dark hair. "Wow, what a big crowd! My arm is hurting from all that salsa scooping, and we've still got a long way to go. Elena said that most of her high school class is coming to the second show."

"Time to clean up, Team Cowgirl!" Maeve announced, adjusting her cowgirl hat and doing a little spin in her boots. *Only Maeve could pull off an outfit like that,* thought Charlotte.

The girls heard the slamming of car doors outside and saw a group of people moving toward the ticket counter. "Wait a minute, guys," Avery said, uncovering the baskets of tortilla chips. "Last-minute surge."

A crowd of about twenty kids filed into the Movie House, tickets in hand.

Charlotte elbowed Avery. "Warning! QOM alert," she whispered, just loud enough for all the BSG to hear.

The five girls looked up to see Anna McMasters and Joline Kaminsky, Abigail Adams Junior High's resident Queens of Mean, coming their way.

Avery straightened her bandana as they approached. Maeve had decided that if they weren't all going to dress up, they could at least wear Charlotte's red bandanas around their necks, cowboy-style.

Anna and Joline approached the table and sniffed tentatively at the food.

"Would you like a mocha chocolate chunk cupcake?" Isabel asked, trying her best to be polite. It wasn't easy, though. Anna and Joline were definitely the meanest girls she knew.

"Thanks, but no thanks," Anna replied with a snort. "I *never* eat bake sale food—it's way too sketchy!"

"Then move along." Charlotte waved her hand. "You're holding up the line."

Anna's mouth dropped open, and Avery thought the girl might actually faint. Charlotte was usually very shy when it came to the QOM.

As soon as Avery collected money and distributed change to the last group of moviegoers, she turned to Charlotte. "*Move along*? You're holding up the *line*? Where did *that* come from? Ten points for Charlotte Ramsey . . . zinger of the week!"

"Did you see the look on Anna's face?" Katani asked, clapping her hands together. "Priceless!" She gave Avery a high five.

"Way to put those two in their place!" Avery gloated.

After they all had a good laugh, it was time to get back to business. "All right, let's take inventory," Katani said.

"And clean up," Charlotte added, running the sweeper over the lobby's red and gold carpet.

"Avery and I can count the money drawer," Katani offered, pulling out her calculator.

"We definitely need more chips. Thankfully, Elena Maria made more salsa than we asked her to," Isabel said as she ripped open a new bag of tortilla chips.

"I can call my mom and ask her to pick up some more chips for the second show," Avery said, as she stacked quarters in piles of four.

Katani was busy counting the bills. When she was done she recounted them—just to be safe—and a wide smile spread across her face.

"I don't believe this!" Katani shouted.

"What?" Maeve asked, completely startled by Katani's sudden outburst.

"What is it, Katani?" Isabel demanded.

"We've already made two hundred and seventy-five dollars! Even if the second show is half what the first show was, we'll still have more than enough. Maeve and Isabel, there's no doubt about it—we're ALL going to Montana!"

The music from the opening credits drifted out the theater doors and came to a well-timed crescendo.

"All for one. And one for all!" Avery shouted.

"Yeeeeee haaaaawww!" Maeve cried, tossing her cowgirl hat in the air.

5

Above the Clouds

Fashionista Katani found herself ooohing and ahhh-ing when Maeve bounced out the door of her apart-ment and onto the sidewalk outside the Movie House, where a van stuffed with the BSG, Mr. Ramsey, and all their luggage was waiting. "And you were freaking out about what to wear! You look like you stepped right out of the Sundance Film Festival!" Katani exclaimed. "I'm very impressed!"

Isabel was instantly drawn to Maeve's sensational pink outfit—scrunched magenta suede boots over pale pink tights and a multipink plaid mini skirt with a swingy bubble hem. She wore a classic white shirt under her pink and burgundy plaid wool jacket. The ensem-ble was topped off with a newsboy hat that matched the plaid jacket.

Maeve was totally put together in a head-to-toe "look at me" way that only she could pull off.

"Check it out! Cool redhead in pink!" Katani called.

Maeve grinned as she spun around like she was posing for a camera.

"If I were a fashion editor, that's the caption I'd write under your picture," Charlotte added, giving Katani an approving nod.

Avery was the only one who seemed unimpressed by Maeve's outfit. "Geez, Maeve. Looks like you fell into a bottle of Pepto Bismol," she joked. "Ew . . . you know, that stuff people take when their stomach is upset?"

Maeve pretended to look furious as she hopped into the van. "Thanks a lot."

Avery laughed and threw her arm over her friend's shoulder as the van rumbled through the famous Callahan tunnel on the way to Logan Airport.

When they arrived, Maeve strutted through the lobby like a Hollywood starlet with her own personal entourage. After lots of walking, waiting, and standing in line, the BSG finally made it to the gate just in time to board the plane. Charlotte and her dad had seats in business class (courtesy of the magazine), while Avery, Maeve, and Isabel shared a row in coach with Katani just across the aisle.

Maeve and Katani were the only two who had never been on a plane before, but both insisted they didn't want the window seat. "I can't. I just can't! I'll seriously freak," Maeve squeaked. Poor Maeve gripped both armrests during takeoff and looked a ghostly shade of white.

"Are you okay?" Isabel asked above the roar of the engines as the plane lifted off the runway.

"Uh-huh . . . super!" Maeve answered with a nervous laugh. But when the pilot came on the intercom and announced they were flying at 30,000 feet, a look of complete horror struck her face.

"Thirty thousand feet?! But that's impossible!" Maeve insisted. "Isn't that too high? How can we breathe?" she asked, putting her hands over her lungs and gasping for air.

"Shhhhh." Isabel patted Maeve's arm. "It's okay, Maeve. Just, um, breathe normally. See? Like everyone else. People fly every day."

Maeve looked around and slowly calmed down a bit. But when the plane hit a patch of turbulence over the Great Lakes, she totally lost it.

"Why is the plane shaking? We're going down!" Maeve shrieked. "I've got to call my parents and tell them I love them!"

Katani ducked her head into her magazine as other passengers craned their necks to check out the commotion Maeve was causing.

"Maeve, relax. It's just turbulence," Avery interrupted. "It's a normal part of flying."

"Turbulence?" Maeve sniffed fearfully. "That sounds like a bad thing."

"It's air currents," Katani explained. "Simple science."

"Well, it feels like we're being sucked into a tornado. Are we falling? It feels like we're falling!" Maeve grabbed Isabel's arm and squeezed her eyes shut.

"Geez, Maeve, relax," Avery said. "This is nothing. You should try visiting my dad in Colorado. Flying through those mountains is like a roller coaster ride."

Isabel gave Avery a stern look. Sensitivity wasn't always Avery's strong point.

"Excuse me, miss. May I bring you something?" a passing flight attendant offered.

"How about a train ride to Montana instead?" Maeve tried to laugh.

"Oh, don't worry. Everything is fine," the flight attendant assured Maeve as she patted her shoulder and handed her a bottle of water.

"Take deep breaths," Isabel suggested after the flight attendant continued down the aisle.

Maeve gasped dramatically a few times. "I can't breathe. Are you sure we have oxygen? My head is spinning. Can't you feel it, Isabel? This is it! I know it is!"

"Shhh," Katani whispered from across the aisle. "Maeve, you have got to chill out!"

"Excuse me, young lady?" The girls looked up to see a very handsome man in uniform standing in the aisle between them.

"I wanted to give you my personal assurance that the plane is completely, a hundred percent safe." The man smiled as he kneeled next to Maeve's seat. "Part of my job as copilot is to stay in contact with the tower and air traffic control. We can change our altitude to avoid bad weather. No need to worry about a thing."

Maeve began to breathe more normally and loosened her grip on the armrest.

"Feeling better?" he asked.

Maeve nodded and flashed him a sheepish grin.

He offered his hand and Maeve shook it.

"I'm Captain Aaron Olcrest. It was very nice meeting you, Miss . . ."

"Uhh . . . Maeve Kaplan-Taylor," Maeve blurted.

"Okay, then, Maeve Kaplan-Taylor. I hope you enjoy the rest of your flight." He gave Maeve's hand a friendly squeeze and tipped his hat.

Isabel looked at Maeve, who flashed the copilot a dazzling smile.

After he left, Maeve relaxed back into her seat and fanned her face with her in-flight magazine. "His cologne was intoxicating," she yawned before falling asleep on Isabel's shoulder.

Montana at Last!

After they deplaned, the BSG made their way into the small Bozeman, Montana airport. Inside the terminal, they made a beeline for the bathroom, while Mr. Ramsey stood guard over their belongings. "You can freshen up, girls, but be quick about it." Mr. Ramsey tapped his watch. "Regional airports are usually pretty fast with the luggage."

As they left the restroom, the girls stopped at the window to take a look around at the Montana scene. Most of the people at the airport were in jeans and plaid shirts, and some were even wearing cowboy hats and boots. Maeve clearly stood out in her pink creation and seemed to drink in the attention—in the form of stares—she was getting from other people around her. In fact, she was beaming. It was as if she thought everyone in the airport was part of her personal fan club.

"Wow," Avery marveled, looking at the dramatic scenery outside the large windows. "Those mountains are huge!"

"I think those are the Bridger Mountains," Charlotte informed her. "And those are the Spanish Peaks," she continued, pointing. "That's where the resort is. I looked it up online."

"Cool!" Avery responded, pressing her face against the window to get a full view of the mountain ranges. The white-capped peaks sprang up from the valley floor and seemed to go on in both directions indefinitely.

Meanwhile, Maeve was distracted by a different sort of view. "What do you think *that's* about?" she whispered to Katani, directing her attention to their right.

Katani looked to where Maeve was pointing. Mr. Ramsey, surrounded by all their carry-on bags, was talking to a woman in a snappy leopard print coat.

"She's pretty!" Isabel blurted.

"Looks like *someone* has found something *other* than the beautiful scenery to admire," Maeve said in a singsong voice.

Katani sighed. "Maeve, you have a one-track mind. Just because Mr. Ramsey is talking to a woman doesn't mean anything."

"We'll *see*," Maeve replied, giving Katani a meaningful look.

Star Sighting

At baggage claim, the light started flashing, an alarm bell rang, and the conveyor belt lurched into operation. Maeve couldn't see anything through the throng of people ambushing the conveyor. Suddenly, Charlotte popped out with a bag in each hand, which she placed at her father's feet before worming her way back through the crowd to find the rest.

"How did she do that so fast?" Maeve wondered. "My mother's black suitcase looks just like everyone else's!"

But Charlotte Ramsey had done enough world traveling to know that a bright polka dotted ribbon tied to the handle of her bag was a very helpful trick when it came to spotting her luggage.

"Wish I'd thought of that," Katani said enviously.

Maeve was impressed. Once she became an actress and was traveling all over the world for movies and premieres and whatnot, she would have bright pink luggage, or maybe leopard print luggage, something that would stand out as being totally HER. Maybe she would get her own initials in gold—MKT. Or would that be too much?

Charlotte surfaced from the crowd with two more bags—Katani's stylish rolling suitcase and her dad's big duffel. She looked around for her dad and noticed that he was still talking to the woman in the leopard jacket.

"Girls, this is Lissie McMillan," Mr. Ramsey announced as he rejoined the group. Ms. McMillan looked dazzling. Her honey-colored hair with golden highlights hung stylishly around her heart-shaped face. She had an easy, engaging smile and eyes that were large, distinctively yellow-brown, and captivating. She wore expertly applied eyeliner, which made her eyes look even more catlike.

"Nice to meet you all. I guess I should get my bag," Ms. McMillan said. "Be right back."

The group was a little dumbfounded as they observed Mr. Ramsey watch her walk away. "Ms. McMillan has decided to give up her job in a Boston brokerage house to return to her western roots. Her mother's family came from Montana, and—get this—she's going to be working for the next few months at Big Sky Resort. Can you believe it? What a small world!" Mr. Ramsey exclaimed.

The group was silent.

Dad is acting kind of weird, Charlotte thought.

"I suggested that since I rented a van with so much extra room, Lissie should ride with us," Mr. Ramsey informed them.

Mr. Ramsey looked up to see Lissie pulling a large suitcase off the conveyor. "Here, let me help you with that." He rushed to the belt to haul the suitcase off.

Maeve gave Katani a look.

"Don't say anything!" Katani warned Maeve. "Just because he offered her a ride doesn't mean he's in love with her. Hello? Maeve? I'm talking to you! Oh, what now?"

Maeve was looking past Katani, wide-eyed and incredulous. "Omigosh," she managed to gasp. "OH MY GOSH. It's Nik!"

"Nick Montoya? No way!" Katani exclaimed.

"No! Not Nick Montoya—Nik of Nik and Sam!"

"Nick and *who*?" Katani turned around, expecting to see a couple of guys.

"Did you say Nik and Sam?" Avery asked, whipping around. "Where? WHERE!"

"There!" Maeve pointed, dropping her bags on the floor and sashaying over to where the two were standing.

"Who are Nik and Sam?" asked Katani.

"Come on, don't tell me you've never heard of Nik and

Sam," Avery groaned. "Maeve played their CD for us at the sleepover a few weeks ago. They're twins and country singers from Arkansas. I love them! They're around our age, too."

Katani looked over at the two girls with long, tawny hair. In an instant Maeve was rushing up to their side, talking to them like they were old friends. The rest of the group hung back as Maeve solicited autographs from the two celeb musicians, who seemed to be admiring Maeve's glitzy travel outfit—the pink boots in particular. Maeve pawed through her jumbo pink patent leather bag and then called Charlotte over, motioning that she needed something to write on.

By that time all of the bags had been gathered, so the whole group dragged their suitcases over to Maeve.

"Nik and Sam, these are my best friends: Charlotte, Avery, Katani, and Isabel. And this is Charlotte's father, Mr. Ramsey." Maeve swept her arm across the group. "Oh, yeah. And this is Lissie McMillan. She's Mr. Ramsey's new . . . *friend*," Maeve added.

"Hey, girls," Nik greeted them with a smile and a wave.

"It's nice to meet y'all," said Sam.

Nik and Sam introduced their parents, their agent, and the rest of their entourage to the Beacon Street Girls. Maeve was glowing with excitement, and all the BSG were captivated by the twins' star power and their down-to-earth friendliness.

"It was very nice to meet you all," Mr. Ramsey said, "but I need to go check on our rental car. Stay right here, girls. I'll be back in a second."

The girls didn't have any intention of going anywhere, not when they were having a real-life celebrity encounter!

"We love your music," Maeve gushed. "LOVE it, especially your song 'Old Enough.' It's like you wrote that song just for me!"

"Thanks," Nik said. "It means so much to hear that!"

"So what are you guys doing here in Montana? Don't you live in Arkansas?" asked Avery.

"We're performing at Big Sky Resort this week," Sam replied.

Maeve squealed. "That's where we're going, too!"

"Seriously?" Nik asked.

"Seriously," Maeve assured her.

"That's so cool!" Sam exclaimed. "We were afraid there wouldn't be any girls there to hang out with!"

Maeve beamed. Nik and Sam wanted to hang out with *her*. This week would be even better than she imagined.

Mr. Ramsey returned to say that there was a delay with the rental van and it wouldn't be ready for a few hours.

"Hey, we were planning on having lunch in town before we hit the road for the resort. You guys wanna come?" Sam suggested.

"That's okay, Mom, right?" Nik asked.

"Of course! The more the merrier," Nik and Sam's mom replied with a warm smile.

Maeve grinned from ear to ear, and even Katani, who was new to the Nik and Sam phenomenon, seemed excited to spend some time with the famous duo.

CHAPTER

6

Another World

Charlotte's head was swirling. Although she was an experienced traveler and used to encountering all sorts of delays and unexpected twists, she had never had a surprise celebrity encounter. And now they were about to get into a cab to go have lunch with Nik and Sam at Buffalo Bill's, a swanky western restaurant in downtown Bozeman. That's the thing about travel, Charlotte thought. You never know *what's* going to happen! "Expect the unexpected," her father always said.

Mr. Ramsey wasn't one to get bent out of shape when plans didn't go as expected, but he also wasn't used to looking after five twelve-year-old girls at once. At that moment, Maeve, totally empty-handed, was trailing after the Nik and Sam gang.

"Aren't you forgetting something?" an exasperated Mr. Ramsey called after the starstruck Maeve, who seemed to have forgotten that she was supposed to stay where she was. Sheepish, she made a beeline back to the group. An in-charge Mr. Ramsey corralled everyone and headed them back to the rental car counter explaining, "Girls, we can't drag all this luggage with us."

As the procession of giggling BSG made its way back to the counter, Maeve couldn't resist peering out the window. "There's a *limo* out there," she exclaimed. "The resort sent one for Nik and Sam. Look!" She pointed to a silver stretch limo and a driver holding a sign.

"Whoa," Katani exclaimed. "That's so cool. Nik and Sam, you guys must love riding in an awesome car like that!" she shouted out to the twins, who were waiting by the door.

"We have room for two more people in the limo," Nik and Sam said in unison.

"Yeah, two of you should come with us all the way to the ranch," Sam suggested. "It'll be fun!"

Eyeing the girls' pile of bags, Nik added, "You're welcome to put some of your luggage in the limo, too. We have a little extra room, and it's all going to the same place."

"Thanks!" Maeve said, dragging her bags over to the limo driver who had come inside to retrieve the twins. "Who wants to ride in the limo with me?"

"Wait a minute. Who said *you* get to go with them?" Avery asked.

"It's only fair. You guys wouldn't have even recognized them," Maeve argued. "This is like a dream come true for me."

"I knew who they were, too," Avery pointed out. "We *all* want a limo ride. And anyway, *everything* is a dream come true for you."

"Come on, guys. No fighting," Charlotte pleaded.

"Why don't you draw straws or something?" her father suggested.

Charlotte rummaged through her bag and pulled out four sticks of gum. She tore one in half and handed the five sticks to her dad. "The two that draw the half sticks of gum get to go in the limo," Charlotte explained matter-of-factly.

Katani and Isabel were the lucky winners. Still holding her half stick of gum, Isabel peeked over at Maeve, who looked devastated.

"I can't believe this. Isabel and Katani didn't even know who Nik and Sam were and now they get to ride in their limo? This is just completely unfair," Maeve grumbled.

Charlotte pulled Maeve aside. "Look," she began, hoping that Maeve wasn't going to have a meltdown. "We have a whole week to spend with Nik and Sam. And as far as riding in a limo, someday that'll be part of everyday life for you when you're in Hollywood being famous and fabulous. So let Katani and Isabel enjoy it now."

Maeve smiled weakly. "Okay. Sorry. You're right, Char."

Grizzlies and Ribs

After a short cab ride, the girls were greeted by a big stuffed grizzly when they walked in the front door of Buffalo Bill's Restaurant. The interior was decorated with roughly hewed wood, caribou antler chandeliers, and lots of stuffed creatures.

"Cool! This place is awesome," Avery said, running up

to the grizzly, which towered over her with raised paws and a gaping mouth full of ferocious teeth. She pretended to punch the stuffed grizzly in the stomach and then handed her camera to Charlotte. "Char! Take a picture of me!" Avery cowered as if being attacked by the bear.

"We're meeting some folks," Mr. Ramsey told the hostess as Maeve flung herself into the grizzly picture.

"Here, Charlotte, why don't you join them?" Lissie said. "I'll take the picture." Lissie snapped the shot and handed the camera back to Avery. "That one's a keeper."

The hostess led them to the table to join the group and handed menus to everyone.

"Cool! They have rattlesnake and buffalo on the menu. I can't wait to get home and tell Scott I ate buffalo," Avery exclaimed.

"You're the only one here who *would* eat buffalo," Maeve told her.

"Actually, buffalo is supposed to be very good for you. Fairly low fat, very lean, packed with protein," Lissie said. "And I'm told rattlesnake tastes like chicken, although I've never tried it myself . . . and probably won't." Everyone, including Charlotte, laughed.

"Yum. Throw a little barbecue sauce on that buffalo and it'll be dee-lish," Avery said. "Scott would love this place. This is the kind of thing he wants to do when he opens his own restaurant . . . something with a really cool theme."

"Yeah, Elena Maria too," Isabel agreed.

"Maybe those two can come to Montana on their *honeymoon*," Maeve added, eyes sparkling.

"Not so fast, Romance Girl," Avery held up her hand. "I'm all for Scott and Elena Maria hanging out, but don't get all starry-eyed or anything."

"Hi, I'm Kyle. I'll be your server today," said a handsome young man in worn jeans and a button-down shirt, with a cowboy hat pulled down over his dark eyes. "I'll give you a few minutes to look over the menu." He smiled at the large group and moved on to deliver drinks to another table.

"He's dreamy," Maeve said, gesturing toward the waiter and sighing as she buttered a fresh roll. "Cowboys are *so* my type. I think maybe my future college plans might include the University of Montana."

"Okay, Betsy Fitzgerald," joked Katani.

Maeve made a face. Betsy was their college-obsessed classmate from Abigail Adams Junior High back in Brookline. Maeve hoped she didn't sound like that.

"Kyle *is* cute," Sam agreed.

All the college-aged waiters and waitresses were wearing authentic cowboy gear—hats, cool boots, and snazzy western-style shirts. The servers, along with the authentic decorations and delicious smells, gave Buffalo Bill's a fun, unique atmosphere.

"It'd be great to get some western wear while I'm on this trip, but I know that resort stores can be really expensive. I wonder if there's a good place to shop around here," Katani thought aloud.

One of the waitresses overheard and suggested an inexpensive spot just down the street.

Suddenly, the music cranked up. The waiters put down

their trays and started a choreographed line dance.

"Cool! 'Cotton-eyed Joe!'" Avery shouted.

"Come on!" Maeve grabbed Nik and Sam by the elbows as soon as the waiters motioned for the customers to join in.

All the girls jumped up to test their line dancing skills, and even Mr. Ramsey and Lissie joined the fun. Charlotte and Katani both felt like they had two left feet, but they got the hang of the routine toward the end of the song.

Out of the corner of her eye, Maeve noticed that the twins' father disappeared and returned with two cases. He opened up the cases and began tuning a guitar and a banjo while the dancing went on.

"Here at Buffalo Bill's we are fortunate to have two special people in our restaurant today," Kyle spoke into the microphone at the end of the song.

For a split second Maeve thought Kyle was going to single her out for her dancing skills, but then the waiter gestured to Nik and Sam. Oops, Maeve thought with a blush. *Guess it'll be a couple years before people start recognizing Maeve Kaplan-Taylor in public.*

"Nik and Sam, the country singing sensations, will be performing at Big Sky Resort this week, and we've persuaded them to put on an impromptu performance this afternoon. Let's give Nik and Sam a warm Montana welcome!" Kyle clapped and the crowd joined in, yipping and yelling with the BSG leading the way.

Nik and Sam took their instruments and stepped on stage. They leaned their heads together and whispered for a few seconds, then nodded and faced the audience with bright smiles.

"This is for our new friends from Boston," the twins said in unison before breaking into a soulful noise that immediately got every foot tapping in the house. "They say I'm a wild child . . ." the girls began.

"'Old Enough!' My favorite song!" Avery called out.

By the time Nik and Sam got to the chorus, the BSG were belting out their favorite part: "I'm old enough!"

The song ended and the crowd erupted in ringing applause. Maeve led the BSG cheer, even though she was hoarse from singing with all her might.

"Thank you!" Nik and Sam waved to the audience. "And here's a new one we'd like to share with you," Sam said. The girls slowed down the pace, strumming out a bluesy ballad. "It's just another Sunday morning," the girls crooned.

Mr. Ramsey got up and offered a hand to Lissie, who took it and followed him to the dance floor.

"Hey, Charlotte, your dad is a pretty good dancer," Avery observed. "My dad looks like he's trying to swat and stomp bugs when he dances," she said. "It's definitely not pretty."

"Where did your dad learn to two-step like that?" Katani asked.

"I have no idea," Charlotte replied as she felt a strange knot in the pit of her stomach. She wasn't sure why she felt all shaky and weird inside. It wasn't fear or anger or embarrassment. She just felt uncomfortable.

Meanwhile, all the restaurant goers were exclaiming and trying to get a good look at the twins.

Maeve gave a little wave to some of the onlookers.

Maybe they were trying to catch a glimpse of the one and only Maeve Kaplan-Taylor too. Who knew?

Nik and Sam's dad stood up and announced that it was time to get going. They had to reach the resort in time for the twins to settle in and rehearse before it got too late.

The limo was waiting for them at the front door. Nik and Sam and their parents, along with Isabel and Katani, piled into the shimmering silver car. Katani was a little disappointed that she wouldn't be able to go shopping, but Isabel whispered that she was sure that the resort would have a cool gift shop.

Mr. Ramsey stuck his head through the open window to give the girls some instructions. "All right, girls. Be good, and we'll see you in a bit."

Isabel and Katani nodded.

"When you arrive, tell the person at the front desk that you're part of the Ramsey group. If there is any problem, call my cell. We should only be a half hour to an hour behind you."

Mr. Ramsey stepped away from the limo, and Katani, Isabel, Nik, and Sam waved good-bye to the rest of the group as the limo rolled away from the curb.

"Before we go back to the airport, why don't we check to see when the van will be ready?" Lissie recommended. "No point being stuck at the airport with nothing to do as long as there's a town to explore."

Mr. Ramsey called the car rental place and found out it would be another hour before they could pick up the van.

"Okay, you girls can have a few minutes to shop," Mr.

Ramsey said as he snapped his phone shut. "Do you all have watches?" he asked. "Everyone be back here in fifteen minutes, and stay on this block," he admonished the girls.

The BSG headed down the street, determined to make the most of their fifteen minute speed shopping expedition.

Maeve, of course, had some very important things on her mind: clothes, boots, purses, and accessories. In one word, FASHION! She disappeared into the first trendy clothing shop she found, on the hunt for something totally fabulous.

Charlotte wanted to find the perfect postcard of the Wild Wild West to send to Sophie, her friend in Paris. "I'm heading in here!" Charlotte called as she hurried past Avery and into a drugstore.

Outside the store, Avery discovered a mechanical bucking bronco. "Jackpot!" she shouted. A bucking bronco was much more entertaining than shopping could ever be. Avery jumped on and put two quarters in the slot. "Yee haaaaaawwwww! Charlotte!" she called. "You have to get this on camera."

Charlotte popped back out of the store and grabbed Avery's camera to take a few priceless snapshots. As Avery hooted and hollered and held on for dear life, some people paused to point or chuckle before continuing down the street. Avery didn't mind, though. She was used to people watching her athletic performance.

Charlotte spotted a bookstore across the street and ran over to check their postcard selection. Not only were there some beautiful landscape postcards, but she also found a whole section of cowboy poetry. She was deep into a poem called "Stampede" when her father came through the door.

"Hi, Charlotte. I thought I might find you here," he said. "I just got a call from the rental place, and they have a vehicle for us now. Where are the others?"

Charlotte bought the book of cowboy poetry, and met her father outside to look for Avery and Maeve.

"There's Avery," Charlotte said, pointing across the street. Avery was still hooting and hollering on the bucking bronco. Just as the Ramseys were trying to get her attention, she jumped off and disappeared into a western-wear shop.

Charlotte noticed her dad's exasperated expression. "I think Maeve might be in the shoe shop on this side of the street. Let's get her first and then we'll get Avery."

They found Maeve sitting on a bench inside the shoe shop with boxes and boxes of cowboy boots surrounding her. "So many boots! So little time!" Maeve moaned.

"You've got that right, Maeve. Our van is ready and Big Sky Resort is waiting. Please go pay for your boots and meet us outside." Mr. Ramsey said, pointing at his watch. "Checkout counter . . . now!"

Maeve grabbed a pair of rose-colored cowboy boots, threw them back into the box, and hurried to make her first western purchase.

By the time they made it across the street to the other western shop, Avery was barreling out the door.

Mr. Ramsey caught Avery by the backpack before she

could take off again. "Great," he breathed a sigh of relief. "I finally have you all together. Line up against the wall."

"What?" Maeve asked incredulously.

"You heard me! Line up." Mr. Ramsey looked pretty serious, so the three girls quickly scurried into a line and stood at attention.

"Okay. Left face. That means turn to your left. Your OTHER left, Charlotte. Now, MARCH!"

Mr. Ramsey marched the girls, giggling all the way, back to the front of the restaurant where Lissie was waiting with their luggage. And just in time, too. As Mr. Ramsey shouted "Halt!" to stop the marchers, a cab pulled up in front of the restaurant and they all piled in.

7

Mountain Rovers

W ell, it's certainly *not a limo*," Maeve observed.
The group stood in the parking lot of the car rental place, staring curiously at the strange vehicle that had been assigned to them.

"What *is* it?" Avery asked. She'd never seen a car like this one!

"It's a Mountain Rover," Charlotte said. "A version of the Land Rover. We used them all the time when we were in Africa. They're rugged, but they're not all that reliable, are they, Dad?"

Mr. Ramsey shook his head. "You're right, Charlotte, but the Rover should be just fine for our trip. We don't have too far to go."

"I've never heard of a Mountain Rover." Maeve shook her head, walking around the vehicle and examining it like an exhibit in a museum. "But whatever it is, it's the most disgusting shade of orange I've ever seen."

"What's the matter, Maeve?" Avery asked. "Were you expecting a pink jeep to match your outfit?"

Maeve ignored Avery's joke. "So, it looks a little beat up. Does it run?"

"That's not a bad question." Mr. Ramsey motioned one of the attendants over.

"We're concerned about the condition of our vehicle here," Mr. Ramsey said. "Is it going to make it all the way to Big Sky Resort?"

"Ole Nelly here is an excellent vehicle *and* she has four-wheel drive, a must in these parts," the attendant assured him. "Besides, this is the only vehicle big enough for five people and that mound of luggage. Nelly's been all fired up, and she's ready to go." The man grinned a little too brightly. He looked like he was wishing with all his might that the group would just take off and leave him alone.

"Good thing your bags went in the limo," Avery quipped, tapping Maeve on the shoulder. "We wouldn't have been able to fit your bazillion suitcases in Ole Nelly."

"Well, my bags are riding in *style*," Maeve said. "And that's all that matters." They packed their luggage and piled into Ole Nelly. Mr. Ramsey turned the key in the ignition and the bright orange Rover roared to life.

"Go, Ole Nelly," Charlotte cheered as they pulled away from the rental lot and toward the airport exit. "It's fun having a car with a bit of personality!"

As they headed to the highway, the girls stared out the window and let the two adults in the front seat be their navigators.

"Uh, Richard? You missed the entrance to the interstate," Lissie said. "It was right back there."

Charlotte giggled and then tried to cover it up with a cough. That comment wouldn't get Lissie anywhere. Richard Ramsey was not an interstate driver—at least whenever he could help it. "Dad's more of a back roads type of guy," Charlotte explained.

"*Back* roads," Maeve grumbled. "That sounds like we're taking the long way. By the time we get there and check in, Nik and Sam will be there hours before we will!"

"This view will be worth it, Maeve," Mr. Ramsey counseled her, glancing back in the rearview mirror. "For a while this road follows the Gallatin River, which is supposed to be very scenic. Then when we get to the resort, you'll see a single, huge mountain towering above the rest of the range, right over the resort. They call that Lone Mountain. It's pretty spectacular. And," Mr. Ramsey added, "there's always the chance we could see wildlife on this drive too."

"Wildlife?" Avery repeated, instantly perking up. "Now you're talking."

"All sorts," Mr. Ramsey told her. "Mountain goats, moose, black bears, marmots, mule deer . . . it's all out here."

Maeve shook her head unhappily. "Mountains? Moose? Alpine tundra? And what's a marmot? How do these compare with real life music stars and a luxury resort?" she muttered to herself.

8

Big Sky or Bust

The road rolled out in front of the dude ranch–bound travelers like an endless ribbon of cement, heading west toward the majestic mountains. Occasionally a pickup truck rattled by in the other direction on its way to Bozeman. Charlotte dug her journal out of her backpack and began to write, just words at first, but words that might be later fashioned into a poem: "Hanging clouds looming white, rolling mountains all in sight . . ."

The beautiful scenery even coaxed Maeve out of her dejected mood. "No wonder they call this Big Sky Country," she said, gawking at the scene before her eyes.

"The official nickname is actually the Treasure State," Avery reported.

"Really? What kind of treasure?" Maeve asked.

"Gold and silver. They were discovered here in the eighteen hundreds," Avery told her. "I know lots of stuff about Montana. I read one of my dad's old guide books before we left. Like did you know Montana has the smallest river in the world? It's called the Roe River and it's only like two hundred feet long," Avery rattled off.

"Really? There's actually a river that's only two hundred feet long?" Lissie asked. "That's so tiny."

"Yeah. It's even in the *Guinness Book of World Records*," Avery said.

"Wow, Ave. You're chock-full of Montana trivia. What else have you got?" Charlotte challenged.

"Let's see, the capital of Montana is Helena. And Billings is the largest city in the state, and Yellowstone County is the most populated area in the state."

"Hey, what's Massachusetts' nickname?" Maeve wondered aloud.

"The Bay State," Charlotte piped in. "And Indiana is the Hoosier State."

"Hey! I know a bunch of nicknames too," Avery announced, not wanting to be outdone. "Illinois is the Land of Lincoln."

"Missouri is the Show Me State," Charlotte said.

"Show me what?" Maeve asked.

"Show me how many nicknames you know," Avery responded, cracking up.

"New York City is the Big Apple," Maeve said triumphantly, with a toss of her hair.

"Tanzania is the Cradle of Humankind," Lissie noted.

Charlotte caught her father's eye in the rearview mirror. One of his travel books was about Tanzania. Did Lissie already know this? Most people, unless they lived there or were geography buffs, didn't even know where Tanzania was.

"Well, technically that's the nickname for the Olduvai Gorge," Charlotte clarified.

"The what?" Maeve asked.

Lissie turned around to face Maeve. "The Olduvai Gorge, a deep ravine located in the eastern Serengeti Plains of northern Tanzania," she explained.

Huh, Charlotte thought. *I guess Lissie must be a geography guru.*

"The Great Wall of China is the only man-made structure that you can see from space," Avery threw out.

"Actually, that's just a myth," Charlotte informed her.

"The Great Barrier Reef is the only *living* thing that can be seen from space," Lissie added.

Charlotte's eyes met her father's again in the rearview mirror. This was getting kind of bizarre.

"The water in and around the Great Barrier Reef covers an area just slightly smaller than the state of Minnesota," Charlotte reported.

Lissie whipped around to look at Charlotte. "I can't believe it! You must have read *Serengeti Summer* and *Life on a Coral Reef.*"

"Hasn't everybody?" Charlotte joked, and everyone but Lissie laughed.

Lissie turned around in her seat to face the BSG. "You girls read those books?" she asked. "They're quite advanced for seventh graders."

They all nodded, grins widening on their faces.

"I *love* those books. They're *amazing*," Lissie gushed.

Charlotte looked at her father's face in the mirror. His cheeks were turning bright, fire-engine red.

"Reading travel books is a hobby of mine," Lissie continued. "But so many of them today are just the same old facts over and over again. But those books—those books make you feel like you're actually there."

The interior of the Mountain Rover was momentarily quiet. All that could be heard was the squeak of the seat springs as the old vehicle bounced down the road.

"Do you know what I mean?" Lissie asked.

"Yes, I do," Mr. Ramsey said, smiling a little and looking back at Charlotte through the rearview mirror.

"It's actually one of the reasons I'm here right now," Lissie went on. "Because of the author of those books. Weird, huh, that I would quit my job and start my life over because of some random author?"

"You can say that again," Maeve snickered.

"You quit your job and moved to Montana because of a book on Tanzania?" Avery asked.

"It wasn't because of Tanzania or Australia; it was the spirit of adventure that Richard Ramsey wrote about so eloquently," Lissie explained. "He's really a terrific writer."

"Richard Ramsey, as in my dad, as in the man sitting next to you," Charlotte informed her. Lissie's mouth fell open and she looked like every last breath of air had been sucked from her lungs.

"You're *the* Richard Ramsey?" Lissie looked astounded. "I can't believe it! I never *imagined* I was talking to THE Richard Ramsey!"

Mr. Ramsey nodded and blushed, obviously flattered by the attention.

"I LOVE your books," Lissie gushed.

Charlotte cringed. She couldn't stand the way Lissie made it seem like she was the only one in the universe who loved her dad's books. Charlotte not only loved those books, but she had *lived* them. They weren't just descriptions of places the Ramseys had visited; they were like huge pieces of Charlotte's life.

Mr. Ramsey didn't say anything. By now even the tops of his ears were bright red.

"What inspired you to start writing?" Lissie asked.

That question prompted a long and deep conversation between Lissie and Mr. Ramsey. The two chatted on and on as the car bumped along the road.

"We could have fallen out of the car miles ago and those two wouldn't have noticed," Maeve observed, causing Avery to crack up.

Charlotte didn't think it was so funny. After all, her father had picked this highway for its incredible scenery and views, but he was missing all of its glory because he was too wrapped up in talking to Lissie McMillan.

"Those skies are pretty cloudy," Avery noticed, pointing across the mountain tops.

In just a few minutes the clouds had knitted together and formed a huge, dark cluster.

"Looks like a storm is brewing," Charlotte commented. "Hey, Dad, check out those clouds."

The dark blue-black mass hung so low over the mountain range that some of the white peaks had vanished.

The Mountain Rover hit an extra big bump and

everyone was launched airborne for a second, only held back by their seat belts.

"Cool! This is kind of like a ride at an amusement park," Avery said. "Do that again, Mr. R!"

"I'm going to be black and blue by the time we get to the ranch," Maeve said, rubbing her elbow, which she'd banged against the seat-belt clip.

"Dad, those clouds look pretty ominous to me," Charlotte observed, staring out the window.

"You're right, Charlotte. There's definitely a storm brewing. Looks like snow to me. My grandmother used to talk about the sudden storms that whipped up here in the mountains," Lissie responded.

"Hey, what's that ahead?" Avery asked. Everyone followed her gaze through the front windshield.

The Mountain Rover had reached the crest of the hill where the road dipped into a canyonlike valley. As the car rounded the bend, a quaint western town came into view.

"I bet it's an old mining town!" Charlotte declared.

"This is so cool! A real live ghost town!" Avery exclaimed, staring out the window.

"Like in the movies?" Maeve wondered. "I didn't know ghost towns really existed. I thought they were made up."

"No, they're very real, and you can still find a few in Montana. People flocked here when gold and silver were discovered. Towns sprang up near the mines, but once the gold was gone the people left too. Nothing is left here but the buildings," Lissie explained.

She's obviously been reading up on the West, Charlotte

thought. She had to admit that Lissie sounded like a real adventure guru—and a history buff too.

"And the ghosts . . . what happened to them?" Avery asked with interest.

"Ghosts? Do these places have real ghosts in them?" Maeve wondered.

Avery let out a low, wicked, ghostly laugh.

"Stop it, Avery. You're creeping me out!" Maeve exclaimed, hiding her face in her hands.

"Lissie's right," Mr. Ramsey said. "Once the mines proved unprofitable, all the people moved away. Some mining towns have been turned into tourist destinations."

"I read about one Montana ghost town that's now a state park," Charlotte jumped in.

"Yes, I remember my grandmother talking about Bannack. It's north of here," Lissie said.

"Can we stop, Mr. Ramsey? Aren't you curious to find out what's behind those doors?" Maeve pleaded.

"Sorry, girls, it's getting late, and those clouds look like bad weather closing in quickly. I don't think we can afford to stop." Mr. Ramsey stepped on the gas and the road rose steadily as they rattled out of town.

"What are those yellow poles?" Avery asked.

"Those are to mark the edge of the road so the snowplows won't drive off it," Mr. Ramsey informed her.

"But they're like twelve feet tall!" Avery exclaimed. "Does the snow really get that high?"

"Sure it does!" Lissie said. "My grandmother told me about snowfalls of six feet with drifts up to twenty feet high in some places."

"But that's taller than a house!" Maeve cried.

Lissie nodded. "Yeah. The weather gets pretty intense around here sometimes."

"You don't think it's going to snow that much tonight, do you?" Charlotte asked her dad.

"I hope not!" Lissie responded, as she looked out the window toward the darkening sky.

I wasn't asking YOU, Charlotte thought to herself. Lissie was really getting on her nerves. She seemed to be making herself right at home, and she had only met the BSG a few hours ago!

Mr. Ramsey turned the radio on to find a weather report, but the only station that came in was playing honky-tonk country songs. They were all laughing over the crazy lyrics of one song when the announcer broke in and warned of the oncoming snowstorm.

"A winter weather advisory is in effect for this afternoon. Heavy snow will begin around three p.m. and last through the night. Precipitation to reach between eight and twelve inches in the Bozeman area, and up to eighteen inches in the mountains."

"Ah, well," Mr. Ramsey said. "Nothing we haven't seen before in New England, right, kids? We'll just keep moving and be snug in Big Sky before we know it."

Ole Nelly climbed out of the valley, chugging and straining on the hills as heavy snowflakes began to coat the ground. Suddenly, and without warning, the car started sputtering and stalled out.

Mr. Ramsey carefully steered the car to the side of the road, slowly crunching over gravel before the car rolled to a stop. The inside of the Mountain Rover was completely silent for a moment.

"So how are you at fixing cars, Richard? Tell me you're one of those handy guys," Lissie said.

"Actually, I'm not that bad at diagnosing sick engines. I usually can figure out what's wrong. But being able to *fix* the car is a whole other story," he sighed.

Mr. Ramsey got out of the Mountain Rover and opened the hood. "It's a broken serpentine belt," he shouted.

Lissie pulled her cell phone out of her purse and flipped it open. "Can't call the rental company," she announced. "No signal. I've got no bars at all. Why don't you all check your phones?"

Mr. Ramsey lowered the hood as soft snowflakes began to fall. "Charlotte, bring me the map I put above the visor. The weather's getting worse, and we'll have to figure out where the nearest active town is so we can get some help."

Charlotte jumped out of the car and handed the map to her dad. He unfolded it on top of the hood and studied it carefully. "That's what I was afraid of. There's no town within a thirty-mile radius."

"Except," Charlotte pointed out, "that ghost town we just passed through. That must be only a mile or so away."

Mr. Ramsey paused for a moment, considering their options. As the snow began falling harder, he made a decision. "Girls, Charlotte's right," he agreed. "It's getting dark fast. We'd better get a move on, so grab what you need. The ghost town it is!"

Charlotte wanted to believe that this was all part of the adventure, something she could write about when she got the chance. But it was getting much colder, much windier, and a little too creepy for her taste.

9

Sweet Suite

L ook, there it is!" Isabel exclaimed as the limo pulled
off the main road through a large, impressive gate of
scrolling iron and heavy stone.

In the distance the huge log structure loomed impos-
ingly. The porch posts were real tree trunks and the doors
were made of shining brass. A big brass sign read: WEL-
COME TO BIG SKY RESORT.

Katani leaped out of the limo as soon as it rolled to a
stop and held out her hand to feel the gentle snowflakes that
were beginning to fall. She and Isabel unloaded their suitcases and walked through the entrance with the entire Nik
and Sam entourage surrounding them. The foyer was striking, with gleaming flagstone floors and a vaulted ceiling of
exposed beams and rafters. There was a huge stone fireplace
with a roaring fire, in front of which stood large, overstuffed
leather couches and chairs in a soft butternut-colored leather.
Native American rugs dotted the floor. Everything was comfortable and rustic, but also luxurious and super cool.

"Welcome to Big Sky Resort," said the woman behind the counter.

Katani explained that she and Isabel were with the Richard Ramsey party, which would be arriving shortly. The girls were perfectly willing to wait in the comfy foyer, but they were thrilled when they heard that their suite was ready.

"A suite? We're staying in a suite?!" Isabel exclaimed as she grabbed Katani's hand.

Katani and Isabel waved good-bye to Nik and Sam, who were hanging out on the leather couches while their parents spoke to the concierge.

"Bye, girls!" Sam called. "Come find us later, okay?"

"You bet!" Katani said with a grin. "And thank you again for the great limo ride!"

As soon as they opened the door, Katani and Isabel stood in shock, staring at their spacious suite. Like the foyer, the walls of the suite were rough-hewn log, but the floor was made of highly polished wood planks. One entire wall was a giant window that spanned two floors and was dressed with heavy velvet drapes. A burgundy leather couch that could fit all the BSG, plus Marty and maybe even Nik and Sam, wrapped around two corners of the room and faced a big screen television. Katani couldn't take her eyes off the entertainment unit, which was built into what looked like a covered wagon sticking out of the wall.

"Look! We have our own wood-burning fireplace!" Isabel pointed out.

"And there are little chocolates on the pillows!" Katani marveled happily.

"Would you girls like a fire to take the chill off?" the bellboy asked.

"Sure!" Katani told him as she exchanged a giddy look with Isabel. "Why not?"

While the bellboy lit the fire, Katani and Isabel wandered around the rest of the suite. They peeked in the master bedroom to see a king-size, four-poster bed with beautiful western landscape artwork decorating the walls.

"There's also a loft," the bellboy informed them.

From the main room of the suite, the girls took the circular staircase upstairs and found a wide room with three sets of plush bunk beds, another leather couch, a leather beanbag chair, and a second huge TV.

Isabel flopped onto one of the bunk beds and kicked up her feet.

"Would you like me to open the drapes?" the bellboy called from the bottom of the stairs.

"What?" Katani said distractedly, poking through some of the drawers and cabinets.

The bellboy pushed a button and the drapes that lined the windows opened electronically.

The girls looked up as the light poured in and were completely awestruck at the scene in front of them. Both of them hurried downstairs to get the full top-to-bottom view out the giant window. Framed by the window, the lawn of the ranch stretched out expansively. Lone Mountain was crowned with purple clouds, and the sky sparkled with snowflakes falling in the golden glow of the late afternoon sun.

"It looks like a painting," Isabel whispered.

French doors opened onto a deck that ran the length

of the room. Sitting on the deck was a huge, inviting hot tub.

"We could all fit in here," Katani said, walking outside to peek in the tub.

The bellboy showed them how to turn the spa on and off before he left them to settle in.

"I wish we had our luggage," Katani said. "If I had my swimsuit, I'd jump into the hot tub right now."

"Look, the snow's getting pretty heavy," Isabel observed, pointing out the window.

"Yikes!" Katani said, looking out at the steady flurry of flakes. "I wonder where the others are. They must be almost here by now. I hope the snow isn't a problem for them."

Katani flipped open her cell phone and dialed Charlotte at the touch of a button.

"It went right to voicemail," she told Isabel. "They're probably not getting cell reception on the road."

"I bet they got delayed at the airport," Isabel mused. "Maybe the van wasn't ready on time."

"Maeve is going to flip when she finds out that we're on the same floor as Nik and Sam," Katani said with a grin. "She is *definitely* going to flip."

As if on cue, there was a knock at the door.

Katani looked through the peephole and unlocked the door to welcome Sam, who had changed into a vintage T-shirt and jeans.

"Hey!" Sam said, peeking in the room. "Cool room! Nik and I have some free time now. They have a big game room downstairs. Wanna go check it out?"

Katani and Isabel looked at each other.

"Well, uh," Katani stammered. "I'm not sure we should leave the room."

Nik joined her sister at the door. "Hey, where is everyone else? Shouldn't they be here already?"

"They haven't arrived yet," Isabel said with a shrug.

"They were only supposed to be about thirty minutes behind us," Sam said, checking her watch. Nik disappeared down the hall and returned with her parents.

"Mr. Ramsey and the other girls haven't gotten here yet?" Nik and Sam's mom asked, looking a little concerned.

Isabel shook her head.

"Look, why don't you girls hang out with us until the rest of the group gets here?" Sam suggested again.

"You have your room keys?" Nik and Sam's mom asked the girls.

Both girls nodded, showing her the keys they had stuck in their pockets.

"Okay," she said. "I think it's all right for you to leave the room, as long as you're not wandering around aimlessly. If I know where you are, that will be just fine. Why don't you give me your cell phone numbers?" she said. "We'll stop by the front desk and let them know that I'm responsible for you until the rest of the group arrives."

Downstairs in the lobby, Katani asked the woman at the front desk if she had heard anything from Mr. Ramsey.

"The group must have stopped somewhere. I'm sure there's no need to worry," the concierge explained to them.

Katani nodded. "Where *are* they?" she wondered. It

was obvious to Nik and Sam that both girls were worried. "We were supposed to spend the whole week together."

"I have an idea," Sam piped in. "Why don't we have a sleepover in our suite? We have lots of room and it'd be so fun. We can watch movies and have snacks and everything. And you girls can get your minds off worrying about your friends. I bet they'll even get here in time to join us."

"That's a great idea," Nik and Sam's mom said. "I'll organize the snacks. How do pizza and salad sound, and maybe some nachos to start with and brownies for dessert? The room service menu looked pretty good. You girls run along to the game room and I'll see about getting this party started."

Katani and Isabel smiled gratefully at their new friends.

"Don't worry, we won't leave you guys alone," Nik promised, throwing her arm around Katani's shoulder.

Katani felt a little better. Still, she couldn't help worrying about Charlotte, Maeve, Avery, and Mr. Ramsey. The snow was beginning to come down hard. She hoped they were okay and not buried in a snowdrift somewhere out there in the wilds of Montana.

"Are you worried, too?" Katani asked Isabel.

"Yeah," she admitted. "I'm actually mostly worried that Maeve is going to kill us when she gets here. Imagine spending all this time doing normal, fun stuff with her favorite singers while she's stuck in a snowstorm."

They both couldn't help giggling at that.

10

Danger in Dry Gulch

very cold group reached the old ghost town. Protected from the snow by an overhang on one of the buildings, they were grateful for the worn, gray wood, curved with age at the edges.

Everyone huddled together by the doorway, relieved to be out of the storm at last. They watched as the wind continued to blow and the snow skimmed over the surface of the road.

The only traffic on the street was tumbleweeds and driving snow. The fact that there were no tracks at all was alarming. No one had come into the town since they had passed through.

As the tired group moved down the street, doors and shutters banged with such ferocity that it made them all jump. It was almost as if the town was trying to scare them away.

"It's just the wind," Charlotte whispered to herself.

"Look in here," Avery shouted as she darted through

the open door of the Dry Gulch Barbershop. Avery jumped into one of the barber chairs and began spinning.

"YEEE HAW!" she cried out as if she were back on the bucking bronco and not just in an old barber chair. "This chair is cool and actually pretty comfortable. I want it for my bedroom!"

"Come on, Avery. It's getting dark. We should find some-place with beds or at least blankets," Charlotte said. "As comfortable as that chair is, it won't be fun to sleep in."

Charlotte peered into the abandoned building next door. One of the swinging doors hung by only one hinge, and Charlotte didn't dare push it in for fear it would crash down onto her toes. As the wind blew the doors open with a loud howl, Charlotte caught sight of the dark, dank interior. The emptiness of the place seemed to suck the breath out of her, and something about it sent chills down her spine.

"Look, Char! A jail!" Avery pointed into the window of the next building on the street.

Charlotte snapped out of the chills and followed Avery inside the jail.

"Look! Wanted posters. Yup, Sheriff. He's a right orn'ry cuss!" Avery joked in her best western drawl.

Charlotte gazed back through the sole narrow window of the jail at the gray light of the street. "Come on, Avery. It's getting dark and the snow's not letting up one bit. We'd better find shelter before it's pitch black."

"Let's go, girls," Mr. Ramsey called, poking his head into the jail.

"Can we explore later? Please?!" Avery asked

"We'll see," Mr. Ramsey said, ushering both girls out into the snowy street.

"There it is," he pointed out after they had walked another block. "The Hotel de Paris."

"*C'est magnifique*," Charlotte said. "*Quelle surprise!* To find a slice of Paris here in the Old West . . ."

"Parisian culture was very popular back when this old town was founded," Lissie told them.

"Hope this hotel has some vacancies," Maeve kidded.

"The whole town is vacancy central," Avery marveled.

Something's odd about this place, Charlotte thought as she looked up at the gilded letters painted on the semicircular window above the door of the hotel. Then it hit her—it was quiet. There were no shutters crashing against the side of the building, no doors banging in the wind. The hotel seemed oddly secure and intact compared to the run-down condition of the buildings nearby.

Charlotte half-expected the door to be locked when her father tried it, but it opened right away. Quiet surrounded them as they entered the hotel. Mr. Ramsey shut the door behind them.

It was still cold, even inside. They could see their breath as they talked, but at least it was warmer than being in the wind outdoors.

Mr. Ramsey fished around in his backpack and pulled out a flashlight. The old chairs in the lobby were covered with sheets, making them look like squat, fat ghosts.

"This place looks like someone's been here recently,"

Lissie remarked to Mr. Ramsey, pointing to a kerosene lantern on the check-in desk. "Look," she gestured to a box of kitchen matches beside the lantern.

"Do you know how to light one of those things?" Avery asked.

"I do," Lissie said, taking a match and striking it on the side of the box. She lifted the glass shade of the lamp and carefully lit the wick inside.

It glowed dimly at first, then lit up with a cheery brightness in the gloom.

Lissie cranked the small wheel on the side of the lamp and trimmed the wick back to create a pleasant glow.

"Look," Lissie said as she lifted the lamp from the desk. As Charlotte leaned over to see what Lissie was talking about, she could see distinct handprints and fingerprints on the dusty desk top.

"Eeeek!" Maeve said, pointing at some tiny footprints in the dust next to dark, rice-shaped droppings. "Is that what I think it is?"

"What?" Avery leaned forward to get a closer look.

"What do you think?!" Maeve looked like she wanted to jump on the closest chair or couch she could find. "It's mouse prints! There's no way I'm staying in any mouse-infested place!"

"You want to stay out there?" Avery asked, pointing to the blowing snow outside.

The thick, wavy panes of glass made it seem as if the snow was already piled up to the windows.

"There has to be somewhere else," Maeve pondered, putting a hand to her forehead.

"This is the most solid structure I saw in town," Mr. Ramsey said.

"I'm *sure* someone has been here recently," Lissie repeated. "All the shutters are intact and the handprints . . ." she gestured toward the desk again. "This place is secure and definitely not abandoned."

"I can't imagine anyone living so removed from civilization. That would be a terribly lonely life," Mr. Ramsey said as he shut off the flashlight and took the lantern from Lissie. He walked toward the stairs that curved gracefully behind the desk. "Hello? Is anyone here?" he called out into the darkness of the second floor. "Our car broke down and we're looking for shelter from the storm."

Only the moan of the wind replied.

The girls huddled together as Mr. Ramsey called upstairs again. "Hello?" Before he could get out another word, a loud bang came from the second floor, followed by a gust of frigid wind swirling down the stairs.

The giant gust blew out the flame of the lantern and the group was plunged into darkness.

Charlotte grabbed her father's arm and Avery grabbed Lissie's. Maeve put a hand to her mouth and let out a blood-curdling scream.

Part Two
Snowbound

11

A Long Winter's Night

O kay, everybody. Let's all stay calm. Most likely the howling is just a draft from an open window somewhere," Mr. Ramsey assured the girls as he rubbed his hands together to keep warm.

"Doesn't it always get colder in scary movies right before a ghost shows up?" Avery asked, eyes wide.

"Let's step over here so I can relight the lantern," Mr. Ramsey directed. The group shuffled in one huddled mass to the front desk. Charlotte noticed her father's hands shaking slightly as he tried to strike the match. *Is he cold or afraid?* wondered Charlotte.

"You girls stay here with the lantern. Make sure you keep it out of that draft, away from the stairs. We don't want to use up all the matches," Mr. Ramsey instructed. He took the flashlight out of his pocket and clicked it on. "I'll go upstairs to investigate."

"Dad, don't go up there alone!" Charlotte pleaded.

"Yeah," Avery said with an attempt at bravado. "It's

like when you're watching a scary movie and you want to yell, 'No, don't do it!'"

Just then the howling became louder, and the girls, including Avery, moved closer together.

"I'll go with you," Lissie offered.

"I think you better stay with the girls," Mr. Ramsey hesitated, looking at three frightened faces.

"We're not babies," Avery protested. "I think we can stay down here by ourselves. Besides, I don't think Lissie can scare away any ghosts or anything."

"I don't like ghosts," whispered a shaking Maeve.

Staying downstairs by themselves sounded like a bad idea to Charlotte, but Lissie had already joined Mr. Ramsey at the bottom of the stairs.

The light grew dimmer as Charlotte's dad and Lissie creaked up the old, winding staircase.

Avery inched around the corner of the desk and looked up the stairs. "No ghost attacks yet!" she reported with a grin.

"Avery! Get back here!" Maeve said in a loud whisper. "Charlotte's dad said we're supposed to stay out of the draft. What are you talking about anyway? Ghosts don't attack people. They just *haunt*."

"Do you know that for sure, Maeve?" Avery asked. "Have you ever met a ghost? Maybe the ones here in Dry Gulch are extra creepy. Remember, there were a lot of bad guys in the Old West."

"Shhhh!" Charlotte demanded, cocking her head.

After a moment of tense silence, Avery couldn't stand it anymore. "Well, at least they're not screaming in terror," she blurted out.

"SHHHHHH!" Maeve and Charlotte shushed her at the same time.

Avery made a face and folded her arms across her chest. She was tired of being shushed.

Finally there were noises from upstairs. A window slid firmly shut. A *swish* of curtains. Instantly the eerie howling stopped.

Charlotte gasped. She hadn't realized she had been holding her breath until that very moment.

"So it was the wind all along and not a real ghost?" Avery asked, obviously disappointed.

"Avery, you really thought it was a ghost?" Maeve asked her.

"No," Avery shook her head slowly, "I thought it was a gigantic mouse!"

"EWWWWWW! Gross!" Maeve cried. Ever since a mouse ran across her hair at the first BSG sleepover, the thought of mice sent Maeve into panic mode.

A sudden and very loud noise from upstairs captured everyone's attention.

"What was that?" A trembling Maeve grabbed Charlotte's hand.

"Maybe it's a body being dragged across the floor," Avery said.

"Your dad's still doing something up there, right?" Maeve asked Charlotte.

"Yeah, I'm sure he is," Charlotte said, patting Maeve's arm. She wasn't sure who she was trying to comfort more — Maeve or herself.

Just then, a beam of light bounced off the wall and

shined into their eyes. The collective scream from all three girls rattled all the windows.

"It's just Mr. Ramsey and Lissie," Avery yelled a little too loudly.

Charlotte was so happy to see her father that she ran up and gave him a big hug. His hands were full with a huge pile of blankets and pillows, and he dropped them on the spot. Lissie had the flashlight, and an unlit kerosene lamp dangled from Mr. Ramsey's right arm.

"So . . . what's the story?" Avery asked.

"Well, the wind was blowing in through the west window. It was only open a crack, which is why it howled and whistled so loudly. It'll be a little warmer down here now that we've stopped that draft."

"But I'm still frrrreezing," Maeve chattered, blowing out a cloud of breath.

"These will help with that," Lissie said.

"You don't think there are any mice in those blankets, do you?" a shaky Maeve asked, backing away slowly.

"No. These blankets were in a trunk, Maeve. A mouse-proof trunk, I'm sure," Mr. Ramsey assured her.

"So what's up there?" Avery asked, obviously itching to know about any gruesome discoveries.

"It's very odd. We went into all the rooms and . . ." Lissie started.

"And what?" Avery asked impatiently.

"And the beds in the bedrooms were all made up," Mr. Ramsey said.

"Really? That's weird," Charlotte mused.

"Yes, it's almost like . . ." Lissie trailed off.

"Almost like WHAT?" Avery asked, her patience wearing thin.

"It's almost as if someone's been living here," Lissie mused, looking around the lobby.

"Living *here*? Are you serious?" Maeve shuddered.

"The sheets are worn, but clean. They seem like they're in fairly good shape and recently laundered," Lissie reported.

The girls looked at each other. "No wonder it feels like there are ghosts all around us. We're trespassing," Charlotte said.

"What if whoever lives here comes back and is mad that we broke in?" Maeve wondered. "You know, sort of like Goldilocks and the three bears?"

"We didn't break in," Mr. Ramsey corrected her. "The door was open."

"But if this hotel belongs to someone else, where are they?" Maeve wondered out loud.

"Let's see what's in the parlor," said Mr. Ramsey a little too cheerfully. Trooping after him into what appeared to be the old hotel's large common sitting room, everyone breathed a sigh of relief.

They found more pieces of furniture covered with sheets—a couch and two chairs facing the fireplace. Logs and kindling were laid out and plenty of wood was stacked up next to a large stone fireplace. It did look pretty inviting.

"Lissie must be right! Someone is definitely living here," Maeve confirmed.

"I don't think so," Mr. Ramsey said as he knelt before

the fireplace with the box of matches in hand. "It looks to me like whoever was staying here isn't anymore. We might as well make ourselves comfortable. We should get a fire going and see if we can find something to eat besides Avery's granola bars."

Mr. Ramsey struck a match and held it to the dry kindling. With a little blowing and coaxing, the fire crackled to life. Charlotte breathed in the comforting aroma of woodsmoke. The glow of the fire and snap and pop of the wood gave the chilly, dank room a little cheer.

"Lissie and Charlotte, why don't you explore the kitchen and see if there are any emergency provisions? After I warm my hands up a bit, I think I'll drag a couple of the mattresses downstairs. We can all camp out in front of the fire," Mr. Ramsey said. "You know . . . like a sleepover."

"Can I go exploring too?" Avery asked.

"Sure, Avery. As long as you stay in the house."

Maeve was happy to crouch next to the cozy fire as the others wandered off to look around.

When they walked into the old kitchen, Charlotte was surprised at what they found. "Look at this! A real French kitchen in the middle of Montana. Maybe the Hotel de Paris really was built by a Frenchman."

"What's so French about it?" Avery asked.

"Well, first of all, the worktable has a marble top," Charlotte pointed out.

"That means it's French?" Avery asked.

"Just trust me . . . it does," Charlotte assured her. Having lived in Paris for several years, Charlotte was attuned to all things French.

The hungry trio couldn't find any food in the kitchen, but they hit the jackpot when they ventured into the pantry.

"Look! Bottles of spring water." Charlotte gathered one under each arm.

"Instant coffee," Lissie sighed with relief.

"And check out this stash of canned goods," Charlotte said, turning the cans so she could read the labels. "Pork and beans, chili and beans, and pinto beans. Someone really likes beans around here."

"Score big time! Look what I found!" Avery hoisted a huge, unopened restaurant-size container of peanut butter and a package of graham crackers in the air.

Lissie checked all the expiration dates. "Great . . . everything's still safe and usable."

They loaded up the canned goods, water, and instant coffee into a large basket.

"Wait! We need a can opener," Avery remembered.

"Here." Lissie held up an odd-looking contraption.

"That doesn't look like any can opener I've ever seen." Avery looked skeptical.

"Trust me. It's an old-fashioned kind," Lissie said.

"But what are we going to cook all this in?" Charlotte asked as she opened up some of the cabinets.

"Look, here's a skillet with legs." Avery dragged it from beneath the sink.

"They call that a spider, I think. It's perfect," Lissie said, lifting it. "Whoa! It's heavy."

"We struck gold," Avery announced as they returned to the parlor.

"Are you sure it's okay if we use this stuff?" Maeve

asked as Mr. Ramsey jabbed the pointed part of the can opener in the can and worked it around the top. "It's not going to make us sick, is it?"

"None of it has expired," Lissie assured her. "Be careful, Richard. The jagged edges are lethal."

While the girls opened the peanut butter, Lissie poured several cans of beans into the skillet. The delicious fragrance of the cooking beans wafted through the air and made their mouths water. Mr. Ramsey disappeared into the kitchen and returned with a pile of metal coffee cups and spoons.

Lissie went outside and scooped up a bucketful of snow. "No use wasting bottled water on dishwashing duties," she said, hooking a bucket so that it dangled just above the fire. Once the snow melted and was steaming, she loaded the bucket with the metal cups and spoons and washed them out. "We really need to let them boil for a bit to make sure they're clean."

Ten minutes later everyone had mugs full of hot, steaming beans.

"I never knew beans could taste so delightful!" Maeve exclaimed, savoring every morsel and licking her spoon clean at the end.

"I saved the best for last," Lissie announced. "Chocolate!" She held two huge Hershey bars above her head victoriously.

Maeve almost swooned.

"Where did that come from?" Charlotte asked, her mouth watering.

"It was in the pantry on the very top shelf," Lissie

answered. "I wanted to surprise you!" Lissie's yellow-brown eyes glistened happily in the firelight.

"Yay! We can make s'mores. S'mores! S'mores!" Avery chanted gleefully.

"Well, we have the graham crackers and the chocolate, but no marshmallows." Lissie shrugged her shoulders.

"What kind of hotel is this?" Maeve joked. "S'mores are a must-have."

"That's it! I want to speak to the manager right now!" Avery giggled.

"Wait. I have an idea!" Maeve pulled out her stash of Swedish Fish. "These might work."

"What! Are you crazy?" Avery asked.

"Trust me," Maeve said. She took a few Swedish Fish and stacked them in an empty metal mug, which she placed on top of the red-hot coals.

A few moments later, Maeve carefully tested the fish with her finger. "Perfect," she determined. "Just ooooey-goooeeey enough." She assembled the strange s'more with confidence.

"Open wide," Maeve told Avery.

"Why do I have to be the first one to try it?" Avery asked suspiciously.

"Oh, please . . . don't tell me you're *scared*?" Maeve egged her on. "Not the great Avery Madden."

"I'm not scared," Avery said.

"Then be quiet and open your mouth!" Maeve urged.

"Here goes nothing," Avery murmured before opening her mouth wide.

Maeve held out the s'more and Avery took a big bite.

"Yum! It tastes exactly like a s'more. No, it's better! Maeve, you're a genius!" Avery exclaimed as she snatched the rest of the s'more from Maeve's hand and gobbled it up.

"But we can't just call it a s'more. It needs another name," Maeve said.

"How about a s'fishmore?" Charlotte suggested.

"That's it!" Maeve said. "We'll have to make a huge box and send them to whoever owns this hotel as a thank-you."

"Well, I'm not completely convinced that anyone lives here. But if someone does, who do you think it is?" Mr. Ramsey asked, raising his eyebrows up and down.

"Maybe they're bank robbers hiding out from the law," Avery speculated.

"Hope not!" Charlotte replied, licking some melted chocolate from her fingers. "Maybe it's a writer—a western writer who wants to get in the spirit of the Old West by living in this ghost town."

"No. No. NO! You're both wrong," Maeve insisted. "It's probably someone who lost his only love and rather than going out into the world, hides out here trying to mend his broken heart."

"Eeew! Why does everything have to be about love and romance with you?" Avery groaned.

"Maeve is what writers call a hopeless romantic," Charlotte explained to Lissie.

"Hope*ful* romantic," Maeve corrected Charlotte. "And very proud of it!" she asserted.

Lissie set the dinner dishes in boiling water and then poured drinking water into the coffeepot. She placed the pot over a bed of red hot coals she had raked to the side of the fire and waited until steam came shooting from the spout. Then she poured the steaming water into two mugs and stirred in instant coffee.

Mr. Ramsey accepted his mug eagerly. "Ahhh!" he said after the first sip. "Warms you from the inside out."

"I have an idea," Lissie said when her mug was almost empty. "Let's play animal charades. It's like normal charades—when you act out a word or phrase—but instead you have to act out an animal. But you can't make sounds! That makes it too easy. Here, I'll start."

Lissie pretended to lick her balled-up hand and then rubbed it over her face to clean herself. Charlotte thought she looked exactly like Orangina, the cat that had lived on her houseboat in Paris.

"A cat!" Charlotte shouted out.

"You got it! You're up next," Lissie said.

Charlotte thought for a minute, then stood up. She folded her arms, tucking her hands inside her armpits to make wings.

"Bird!" Avery shouted.

Charlotte stretched her neck longer. She tried to remember exactly how the largest bird in the world looked on the plains of the Serengeti.

"Chicken," Mr. Ramsey guessed.

Charlotte shook her head and motioned to her lengthened neck.

"Giraffe," Maeve called out.

Charlotte shook her head again and emphasized the flapping of her wings.

"Swan!" Avery shouted.

Charlotte ran around the couch, slapping her feet on the floor to show their large size.

"Ostrich!" Maeve made one more guess.

"Yup, that's it. Your turn."

Maeve scrunched up into a small, compact shape. She wiggled her nose up and down and side to side.

"A mouse," Avery grinned.

"Eeew, ick! Absolutely NOT!" Maeve cried.

"We're playing charades," Avery reminded her. "You aren't supposed to talk."

Maeve fell back into character . . . a small shape with a wiggling nose. She scampered over to Avery and gave her whisker kisses on her cheek.

"Romeo and Juliet," Avery giggled and batted Maeve away from her.

"Huh?" Lissie asked.

"Maeve's guinea pigs," Avery explained.

"You named your guinea pigs Romeo and Juliet?" Lissie asked.

"Actually, I'm calling them Marcia and Jan this week. But you're still right, Avery. I'm a guinea pig."

Avery didn't need to be reminded it was her turn. She jumped on the couch and crouched down. Her knees were sticking up and her arms were resting in her lap. She opened her mouth and stuck out her tongue, then quickly brought it back in. Then she pretended to catch something with her tongue and swallow it with a big gulp.

Charlotte was trying to choke out a guess, but she was so busy laughing she couldn't get the word out.

Avery caught another fly with her tongue. As soon as she had swallowed this imaginary treat, she leaped into the air and landed on the old wooden floor with a thud. Even Mr. Ramsey and Lissie couldn't stop laughing. Avery then proceeded to leap-frog over Maeve, who was giggling so hard she couldn't speak.

"A frog! A frog!" Mr. Ramsey finally managed to get out between laughs.

"You got it, Mr. Ramsey," Avery said as she settled on the couch, a human being once again.

"I don't know if I can top that one, but let me see . . ."

Avery had no idea what sort of animal Mr. Ramsey was trying to portray. He moved very slowly, pretended to eat something, and scratched at his beard a lot. Avery wasn't sure if the beard scratching was part of the clue or if Mr. Ramsey's beard was just really itchy.

After a few guesses, Charlotte finally shouted out the right answer: "Wombat!"

"I thought you'd never get it," Mr. Ramsey said, collapsing back against the couch. "I thought I'd remain a wombat for the rest of my days!"

"What's a wombat, anyway?" Maeve asked.

"It's a mammal that lives in Australia, and it looks like a cross between a small pig and a bear. They are totally adorable," Charlotte assured a skeptical Maeve.

Everyone was having so much fun that they kept going for three more rounds. It was hard to tell who was better at animal charades—Avery, with her very convincing portrayal of a frog, or Mr. Ramsey, who became a hulking, snorting, turf-pawing buffalo right before their very eyes.

"I'm exhausted," Lissie announced as she curled up on the couch. "Though I think it's mostly from all the laughing." She dug through her backpack and fished out a stash of sanitizing wipes. "Anybody else need to clean off sticky fingers?"

Maeve wiped her face and then her fingers with the cool cloth. "I feel so much better!" she said.

From the dark, snowy night outside, they heard a deep howl.

"Was that the . . . the *wind*?" Maeve asked.

"Doubtful." Avery shook her head.

"I bet it was a coyote," Charlotte surmised.

"No. Not a coyote. That was a wolf," Avery announced emphatically.

"How can you tell the difference?" Maeve asked.

"A wolf howl sounds deep and mournful," Avery explained. "Almost like a ghost. Coyote howls are higher pitched than wolf howls, and coyotes usually bark or yap."

"How do you know all this?" Lissie asked.

"Avery watches *Animal Planet* all the time—twenty-four seven," Charlotte explained.

Mr. Ramsey smiled and nodded his head, obviously impressed. "Avery, I think you truly have the heart of a wildlife biologist."

Avery found that to be a very comforting thought. She flopped back on the mattress next to Charlotte and imagined herself trekking through the wilderness in search of all sorts of wild creatures. Visions of wolves and coyotes and frogs and wombats carried her blissfully to sleep.

CHAPTER

12

Ranch Romp

"This is so exciting!" Sam exclaimed, throwing a handful of snow at everyone.

"It's amazingly beautiful, isn't it?" Isabel asked, tilting her head way back and catching a couple of cold snowflakes on her tongue.

The girls strapped on their rental skates and took a couple of laps around the resort's ice-skating rink. Nik and Sam, who had never been on ice skates before, clung to each other for dear life. Isabel was the only one who seemed truly comfortable on skates. She glided effortlessly around the rink as Katani, Nik, and Sam shuffled slowly, wobbling back and forth in a humorous and desperate attempt to stay on their feet.

Feeling brave at one point, Nik let go of Sam and Katani and tried to catch up with Isabel. Her feet, however, seemed to have a mind of their own, each going in a different, unhelpful direction.

"Whoa!" Nik cried out, windmilling her arms as she

desperately tried to keep her balance, but ultimately teetering and collapsing in a heap just as Katani and Sam skated up to her.

"Watch out! Oh, no!" Sam cried, unable to steer herself away from her twin.

Katani and Sam clutched each other, closed their eyes, and screamed helplessly. Katani fell on top of Nik, and Sam catapulted forward, somersaulted over her sister and landed sprawled on the ice.

"Oh my gosh! Are you okay?!" Isabel skated up and helped each of her fallen friends to their feet.

"My ankles are killing me!" Katani declared.

"I think we could all use some hot chocolate," Isabel said, clasping her mittened hands together.

"I could use a pillow," Sam moaned, rubbing her bruised backside.

"MMMMMM! Hot chocolate! That's sounds like an excellent plan," Nik agreed. "Let's get inside before we freeze. Arkansas girls are NOT used to weather like this."

Just next door was a little café open for snacks. Sam went to the counter and ordered four hot chocolates with marshmallows and whipped cream as the rest of the girls settled in front of the fire.

The place was decorated in the same western theme as the rest of the resort, with a rough stone floor and mammoth timbers. Katani couldn't help feeling like she was back in the 1800s.

Moments later, the waiter brought their hot chocolate, steaming and smelling absolutely delicious. Katani wrapped her hands around the cup and inhaled the rich, chocolately scent.

"My fingers are numb!" Nik cried. "Hope they thaw out before our show!"

"I can't remember the last time we had hot chocolate," Sam said. "It's not usually hot chocolate weather in Arkansas. Bet you drink this stuff a lot in Boston!"

Isabel smiled. "We get hot chocolate from our favorite bakery all the time, at least in the fall and winter."

As Isabel launched into a description of Montoya's Bakery, Katani couldn't help starting to worry again about the rest of the group. She hoped that wherever the rest of the BSG were, they were warm and safe.

"You guys play pool?" Sam asked when they had finished their drinks.

"I've played a couple times with my sisters," Katani answered. "How 'bout you, Isabel?"

Isabel shook her head. "Nope, not me."

"I saw they had pool tables in the game room. Wanna give it a try?" Nik asked.

"Sure, why not?" Isabel shrugged. "As long as you guys don't mind teaching me."

"No problem, Iz," Nik assured her. "It's easy!"

The game room at Big Sky was a long, large room that was warm and inviting. A fire crackled in the huge stone fireplace. There were thick, plush brown rugs scattered across the polished stone floor. Two pool tables and an air hockey table stood in the center of the room, while a fringe of video games lined the walls. Snack and drink machines stood in the far corner.

"Howdy," a tall, dark-haired girl greeted them. She introduced herself as Jasmine, one of the teen guide staff members. "Are you all interested in playing a game of pool?" she asked.

The girls nodded and Jasmine handed out the cues, balls, and a rack.

"I'm not that great at sports," Katani hesitated.

"It's all about hand-eye coordination. I'd be happy to show you a few tricks," said a deep voice. Katani turned to see a tall, good-looking boy standing behind her. He took the pool cue from Katani's hand.

"The important thing about pool," he said, "is how you hold the cue and line up the shot." He eyed the table from a couple of angles, lined up the shot, and smoothly hit the cue ball with the stick, which knocked the number 2 ball into the corner pocket.

Nik clapped her hands. "Hey, good one, dude!"

"My name is Daniel." He smiled an adorable, lopsided grin and then handed the pool cue back to Katani. "Now you try," he encouraged her. "Go ahead. You'll do fine."

Katani put her hand on the table and placed the cue on top of it, trying to imitate what she'd just observed.

"Wait. Hold on a sec," Daniel motioned as Katani fumbled with the cue. "Let me show you how to adjust it."

Katani was suddenly aware of how close Daniel was standing to her. He smelled kind of like woodsmoke, fresh air, and spearmint gum at the same time—a strange combination of scents that was making her a little dizzy. She could barely listen to his directions.

"Put your left hand on the table," Daniel instructed.

Katani put her hand on the table, and Daniel placed his hand over hers. Katani could hardly breathe. Daniel had now taken hold of *both* of her hands to position the cue correctly. He spoke softly into her left ear.

"Relax. RELAX! Your left hand is just a guide for you to rest the cue on. It doesn't have to do any work. Now line up the shot. When you're ready, try to hit the cue ball right in the center so it will roll straight. You're pretty close, so you don't want to hit the cue ball too hard. Just a soft tap," he directed. "There, the shot's all lined up. Pull the cue back as straight as you can and bring it forward straight."

Katani did as he said, and the chalked tip of the cue hit the cue ball. The cue ball hit the number 5 ball with a clink and it rolled forward into the corner pocket.

"Yes!" Katani exclaimed, accepting a high five from her new teacher, Daniel.

"You did it," Isabel beamed.

"Awesome," Nik concurred.

"Totally awesome," Daniel agreed and flashed his lop-sided grin. "You've played before."

Katani felt warm and fuzzy all over and snuck a look at Isabel, whose eyes twinkled.

"Hey, over here," Daniel called out to three guys who'd just come through the door. "We were just going to play a couple of rounds," he said to the girls. "Wanna play some speed pool?"

"What's speed pool?" Sam asked.

"Easy. We'll play girls against boys. Each person keeps taking a pool shot until they miss. Three missed shots and you are out! Got it?"

"Got it!" Nik said. "Come on, girls, let's do this!"

"Ladies first," Daniel gestured toward the table with a gallant bow.

"Katani! You're a natural!" Sam exclaimed as Katani managed to sink her first shot.

By the end of the game Katani was surprised to realize that she was the last girl standing. Across from her, Daniel was the last boy.

All the skaters from the ice rink had finished up and come in to check out the game room. The snowboarders had retired for the day, too, and the game room was packed.

"Come on, Daniel! You can take her," a tall boy named Orville called out as the final round began. Katani continued to knock in shot after shot, and to everyone's amazement, including her own, she won the game.

"Woo-hoo!" Katani cheered. "All right!"

"I must be a good teacher," Daniel said with a wink as he high-fived Katani.

What a nice guy, she thought.

"Awesome," Nik proclaimed, also giving Katani an enthusiastic high five.

"You girls going boarding tomorrow?" Daniel asked as he congratulated Katani.

"I don't know," Katani said. "I've never snowboarded before." She wanted to add how klutzy she was at sports, but then thought better of it. They would discover that soon enough when she was tumbling down the mountain.

"Well, if you need a few pointers, let me know," Daniel offered with a smile.

Orville suggested they all meet on the slopes the next day, and the girls agreed.

As she helped put away the pool cues, Katani heard a couple of girls behind her whispering loudly. "Hey, look, isn't that Nik and Sam?"

The buzz started to spread, and soon it seemed that everyone was whispering and pointing to the twins.

Orville was the first to whip out his lift ticket and a pen and ask for an autograph, and then it seemed everyone in the room was scrambling for a scrap of paper. The group pressed closer to Nik and Sam, demanding autographs and shouting out all sorts of questions.

Katani and Isabel were pushed to the side as kids tried to get up close to Nik and Sam.

Nik and Sam were very gracious and open to talking to everyone. Katani couldn't believe how they could stand answering the same questions over and over.

Katani checked her watch. The twins had been fielding questions and signing autographs for quite some time, and they were starting to look tired.

"Nik and Sam," she called out. "Time to go! Sorry, guys," Katani held out a hand to the crowd that clearly meant STOP. "Nik and Sam are late for an appointment. Maybe you can catch them later. Come on, girls," she motioned for Nik and Sam to follow her as she grabbed Isabel's arm. "We gotta get a move on."

Outside the game room, Nik smiled gratefully, then slapped a hand on Katani's shoulder. "Thanks for rescuing us, Katani!"

"Yeah! You should be a band manager or something.

You're really good at getting people to listen," Sam said, slapping her hand on Katani's other shoulder.

Katani smiled. Band manager. She liked the sound of that. As long as the band manager could design costumes and do all that creative stuff, too.

When the girls reached their floor, Nik whipped out her key and unlocked the door to the twins' suite.

"What's this?" Sam asked when she saw how the room had been transformed.

There, in front of the huge window that overlooked the resort lawn and the fabulous backdrop of Lone Mountain, were four sleeping bags with four fluffy pillows.

"Hi, girls," said Nik and Sam's mom. "*This* is a slumber party, Big Sky Resort style. I got the resort concierge to rustle up some sleeping bags to make it more like the real thing."

"A slumber party with a major view!" Isabel exclaimed. She couldn't take her eyes off the majestic, snowy mountain framed by the glow of the moon.

It was fairly dark, but the girls could still see that the snow was swirling and whirling in the darkness between the window and the mountains.

"I hope Mr. Ramsey and the girls are safe," Isabel whispered softly, folding her arms in front of her and shivering a bit.

"Don't worry, Isabel." Nik slung an arm around Isabel's shoulder. "I bet there are a ton of motels and restaurants off the interstate for them to get out of the storm."

Isabel gazed over at Nik's guitar in the corner. Nik followed her gaze. "Do you play the guitar?" she asked

Isabel, jumping at the chance to take Isabel's mind off her worries.

"I've always wanted to take guitar lessons," Isabel admitted. "I can only play a little bit, though—just a few chords."

"Well, there's no time like the present." Sam pushed the guitar in her direction.

"Really?"

"Why not? We only started playing a couple of years ago," Nik said.

She handed Isabel the guitar and picked up the mandolin. Sam began strumming softly on her banjo. Nik patiently showed Isabel some basic chords and then went to get her backup guitar. As they strummed together, all three began to hum sweetly. Sam and Isabel strummed a chord, and Nik broke out in her lonesome, melodic voice, "There's a little girl with a barrette in her hair bouncing on her daddy's knee . . ."

Isabel joined Nik and Sam in the ballad's refrain:

Hold on and don't let go
Put one step forward, two steps back.
No one ever learned to dance without getting just a little off
track.
When your feet get tangled up,
you feel just like a fool
Remember I'll be there taking every little step with you.

"Hey, Katani. Join in!" Sam invited as Nik started in on the second verse.

Katani shook her head and clamped her mouth shut.

"Come on, Katani," Sam tried to convince her. "What's the problem? Just sing along!"

Katani shook her head again and pressed her lips together. She locked eyes with Isabel and the two broke into uncontrollable giggles.

Nik put down her guitar and stared at the two giggling girls. "Is there something weird going on here?" she asked.

Isabel choked back another giggle and shrugged.

"What?" Nik asked.

"WHAT?!" Sam demanded.

"Well, it's just that Katani isn't . . ." Isabel hesitated.

"Isn't what?" Sam pressed.

Katani and Isabel looked at each other and let the giggles flow again.

"Katani is known for her organizational skills, *not* her singing skills," Isabel finally managed to spit out.

"That's putting it mildly!" Katani blurted. "I can't even sing 'Happy Birthday' without making every dog in the neighborhood howl!"

"Come on! You can't be that bad," Sam said.

"Believe me . . . I'm pretty much tone deaf," Katani admitted, shaking her head.

"Well, you didn't think you could play pool, and look how that turned out," Nik reasoned. "Give it a try. You don't have to be a Grammy contender to have a little fun."

"Join in," Sam insisted.

The twins stopped begging and continued to play and

sing, nodding encouragingly at Katani every now and then.

What do I have to lose? Katani thought. She started humming softly at first, then she sang louder and louder, and really let go at the chorus, "Hold on and don't let go. Put one step forward, two steps back. No one ever learned to dance without getting just a little off track."

Five songs later, Katani was belting out the refrain of the twins' foot-stomping jam "Old Enough." Katani knew her voice was terrible and her harmony was way off, but suddenly she didn't care! She sang loudly and proudly, pouring all her emotions into the awesome lyrics.

Isabel and Katani hooted and hollered wildly for Nik and Sam when they finished the song.

"Thank you, everyone, for coming out tonight," Sam spoke to the fake audience.

"We'd like to thank our guest musicians, the talented and beautiful duo, Isabel Martinez and Katani Summers. We couldn't have done it without them both!" Nik added.

By now the light had completely drained from the sky and they could no longer see the white peak of Lone Mountain. There was a knock at the door and a waiter rolled in a cart filled with pizza rolls, buffalo chicken wings, cheese and crackers, a huge bowl of fruit, a plate of cookies, and all sorts of other goodies. The girls put their instruments down and started digging in.

"I might not have a career as a singer," Isabel giggled in between bites of pizza, "but Katani Summers is going to be a *famous* fashion designer someday."

"Really?" Nik asked.

"Aww, we sort of hoped you'd become our manager!" Sam made a funny face.

Katani laughed. "That sounds like fun, but I've always wanted to be a fashion designer. I've already started a scarf-making business, and it's going great. I'm saving all my pennies and dimes and hopefully, by the time I finish college, I'll be all set to launch my fashion empire."

"That's awesome!" Nik and Sam said simultaneously.

"So how did you get interested in music?" Isabel asked.

"We used to go to concerts with our parents where there were guitar pickers. Our dad would always play with them. That's how we started to love music," Nik explained.

"Our dad inspired us first," Sam said, "but I loved Emily Robison, the banjo player from the Dixie Chicks, so I just *had* to learn the banjo. And Nikki learned the guitar so she could accompany me."

"Doing concerts is great, but we'd love to get into acting, too," Sam told them.

Nik nodded in agreement.

"Really?" Katani asked. "Wow, you guys have some big dreams!"

"Tell me about it," Sam laughed. "Someday . . . we want to do a movie too."

"You sound just like Maeve! It would be cool if the three of you were in a movie together," Isabel told them.

"Yeah! Maybe Charlotte can even write the script," Katani suggested.

"Charlotte? Is she a writer?" Nik asked.

"She's a great writer," Isabel reported. "She always has her journal out, and she even writes feature articles for our school newspaper, the *Sentinel*."

"What about you, Isabel?" Sam asked. "What kinds of stuff are you into?"

Isabel looked shyly at the floor and shrugged.

"Come on!" Nik encouraged. "I know you're the creative type."

"Spill it," Sam nudged Isabel.

"Isabel is an artist," Katani bragged.

"Really? Cool!" Sam exclaimed.

"What kind of art?" Nik wanted to know.

"Well, right now birds are my favorite," Isabel said.

"Birds?" Nik and Sam asked in unison.

"Isabel draws these really cool bird cartoons," Katani explained. "She has her own cartoon corner in the *Sentinel*, too."

"You want to be a cartoonist when you're older?" Nik asked, impressed.

"I think I might, but I like other kinds of art, too. I can't decide just yet."

"What other kind of art?" Nik wondered.

"Maybe murals, maybe fabric design with Katani . . . maybe even performance art," Isabel said.

"Performance art! Cool!" Nik exclaimed.

"You don't even know what performance art is!" Sam teased her sister.

"I *do* so know. It's like when an artist is onstage and takes a big balloon full of paint and chucks it at a canvas — sorta like this." Nik picked up the big throw pillow from the couch and lobbed it at her sister, knocking Sam back onto her sleeping bag.

The pillow fight was on.

A Close Encounter

The fire snapped, and Maeve's eyes popped open again. She rolled over and glanced bleary-eyed at her pink watch with the rhinestone-studded face. Only three minutes since the last time she woke up. This time the culprit was a shutter banging against the window upstairs. Even though Maeve was exhausted, every little creak of the old hotel startled her awake. *I am so not a camping kind of girl*, she shuddered.

Lissie and Mr. Ramsey were sleeping in chairs on either side of the fire. Maeve had claimed the old couch— the mouse-free zone—and Charlotte and Avery were sharing a king-size mattress in front of the fire.

Earlier in the evening sleeping on the couch seemed like a brilliant idea. After all, it was high above the floor and less likely to fall victim to a rodent attack. But now, in the middle of the night, Maeve was more worried about the wild animals she heard howling in the distance. Maybe she *would* be safer if she were closer to the fire. Besides, she was shivering in the nippy air.

She took her pillow and blanket and crawled onto the floor. Unfortunately, there wasn't much of a fire left at all. The flames had died down to a mere heap of glowing coals. Maeve maneuvered into the empty space on the mattress between Avery and Charlotte. Suddenly, out of the corner of her eye, she thought she saw a movement in

Trust me, that dude is never going to make it to American Idol.
I'm so lonesome, I could howl.
Isabel M.

the darkness across the room. Was it just her imagination, or was the front door to the hotel actually *opening*?

Maeve squeezed her eyes shut. Of course, it must be her imagination. *Can wolves or coyotes or whatever was making that howling noise open doors*? she wondered, as a shiver went up and down her spine.

Through the tiny slits of her eyelids she saw a dark shadow slowly take shape against the heavy snowfall beyond the open door. A big, scary, tall man with a cowboy hat entered the room.

Maeve clamped her hand over her mouth. If she screamed now, the ghost might swoop her away. She began to shake as the door closed noiselessly behind the silhouette.

As the dark shape began to creep toward her, Maeve reached over and poked Avery's shoulder. She opened her mouth to scream, but only a tiny gasp escaped from her mouth. She shook Avery hard, but Avery wasn't responding.

Suddenly, a howling sound echoed through the room. "Avery! AVERY!" Maeve scream-whispered into her friend's ear. "What IS that?"

"Dreaming. Just dreaming," Avery mumbled and rolled over on her side. Maeve gulped and looked up. There was nothing there, just the grainy darkness. Maeve whipped the blanket over her head and burrowed under the covers.

"I will do my math homework. I will do my math homework. I will do . . ." Maeve repeated over and over again until she fell into a troubled sleep.

13

A New Day in Dry Gulch

Mr. Ramsey put a finger to his lips to let Charlotte know everyone else was still asleep. "Good morning, honey," he whispered.

Charlotte began her super cat stretch and almost immediately discovered she barely had any room to move. On her left, Maeve was sprawled across the previously empty part of the bed. Charlotte inched away from Maeve so she could lie on her back and prop herself up on her elbows without elbowing her friend in the face.

The inside of the old hotel was still dark, but the gray light in the window told Charlotte it was morning. The windowpanes were still. *At least the wind died down a little,* thought Charlotte. But she could still see blustery gusts of snow blowing past the window.

When Charlotte pushed herself up and crept toward the window, a still-sleeping Maeve groaned slightly and instinctively scooted closer to the fire. At the window, Charlotte breathed on the pane of glass and rubbed a spot so she could peer out. Main Street looked like a frozen ocean. The wind had sculpted the snow into great drifts and waves, and in some places it looked very deep. Yet the road was bare in other spots. Charlotte felt it was kind of romantic looking, almost like a great Russian wilderness in the early 1900s. In her mind, she could see the sleds of the proud Cossacks riding down the path.

Charlotte's father had put a pot over the fire, and the smell of brewing coffee was nudging the others awake.

"I wish I had a croissant. After all, this is the Hotel de Paris, isn't it?" a barely awake Maeve asked. "I'll settle for pancakes, though. You are making some of your famous pancakes this morning, right, Mr. Ramsey?"

Avery's eyes fluttered open. "Pancakes? Did someone mention pancakes? My stomach is eating itself," she groaned, sitting up.

"Sorry, girls. No pancakes this morning. I'm afraid it's beans and graham crackers," Mr. Ramsey reported.

"Beans for breakfast? We had beans for dinner! Blah!" Maeve grumbled, pulling the blanket over her head.

"*Someone* woke up on the wrong side of the mattress," Avery joked. "How'd you get here, anyway, Maeve? I thought you were sleeping on the couch."

"I hardly slept all night," Maeve complained, sitting up and stretching.

"I slept fairly soundly myself," Lissie reported. "I bundled up and made a little cocoon with the blankets."

"Then YOU didn't see the ghost," Maeve reported.

"Ghost?!" Charlotte and Lissie exclaimed.

"That's right," Maeve said. "A ghost . . . a real ghost."

"No way. What did this ghost look like?" a skeptical Charlotte asked.

Maeve shivered and looked over her shoulder as she spoke. "He was old. He had white hair and he was wearing this big, long overcoat and a cowboy hat. He looked really mean."

"So it was a cowboy ghost?" Charlotte asked.

"Yeah, a cowboy," Maeve insisted. "I woke up and this guy was opening the front door of the hotel. He stood in the doorway for a while and I could see the snow swirling around behind his head. He looked like one of those old cowboys you see in the movies."

Charlotte just stared intently at Maeve, waiting for her to go on.

"He just stood there for a while and then shut the door and walked, no *floated* toward us. All I know is that one minute he was standing by the door and the next minute he was standing right there," Maeve said, pointing. "Right behind the chair Mr. Ramsey was sleeping in. He was looking down at us. Of course," Maeve dramatically put her hand to her chest, "I pretended to be asleep. Otherwise, I would have had to scream really loud."

Avery scratched her head. "That's weird. I think I had the same dream. A guy standing right there. He was old with white hair. He had on a long overcoat and a big cowboy hat. I dreamed he shook me awake."

"No, that was *me*," Maeve informed her.

"He shook YOU awake?" Avery asked, confused.

"No, I shook you awake. At least, I tried," Maeve said.

"In my dream the cowboy shook me awake," Avery repeated persistently.

"That was no dream, Avery. It was totally real. I shook you awake so you could see the ghost," Maeve told her.

"Why didn't you wake the rest of us up? Why didn't you wake ME up? I've always wanted to see a ghost!" Charlotte exclaimed.

"Well, I closed my eyes for one second—it was so scary—and then he was gone. I swear he disappeared into thin air." Maeve snapped her fingers. "All I did was look over at Avery and when I looked back, he was gone. But I couldn't go back to sleep for a long, long time after that," Maeve said, falling back onto the mattress in exhaustion. "Is it okay if I sleep for the rest of the day?"

"I thought you were hungry," Avery said.

"Uhh . . . right. I'll go back to sleep after breakfast, then." At that point nobody wanted to miss a meal.

"Dad's in the kitchen trying to rustle up something other than beans," Charlotte told the girls.

"I'll go see if he needs any help." Lissie threw on a hoodie over her shirt and went into the kitchen.

When Mr. Ramsey and Lissie returned with armfuls of supplies, Mr. Ramsey announced in his best French accent, "*Bonjour!* Since Mademoiselle Maeve requests no beans, zees morning we are having zee Hotel de Paris delicacy, zee peanut butter and crackers. And for your drinking pleasure, vee have zee boxed milk. *Voilà!*"

"*Dad*," Charlotte groaned. Sometimes her dad could be so embarrassing.

"Boxed milk?" Avery puckered her lips. "Eeeeeeew."

"It is from a very good box, I assure you, Mademoi-selle," joked Mr. Ramsey, offering the milk for inspection. "A very good year."

"I'd give anything for some *chocolate chaud* from a real French bakery," Charlotte said, thinking wistfully of her favorite little café on the *Île Saint-Louis* in the heart of Paris.

"Hot chocolate . . . yum," Maeve said dreamily. "I can taste it now. If my cell phone worked, I'd call Montoya's and ask Nick to make a long distance delivery."

"If your cell phone worked, we wouldn't have spent the night in a ghost town, Maeve," Avery reminded her.

"Look what I found!" an exuberant Lissie cried as she came into the parlor, holding up an ancient-looking frame.

Charlotte squinted, but she couldn't tell what was inside from across the room. She got up to look over Lis-sie's shoulder. "Cool. An old picture."

"I love black-and-white photos. If I were a photog-rapher, I'd only take pictures in black and white," Lissie said.

"Like Ansel Adams?" Mr. Ramsey asked.

"I LOVE Ansel Adams!" Lissie exclaimed, her yellow, catlike eyes glowing as she brought the old photo over for the girls to look at.

"That's HIM!" Maeve gasped.

"Who, Ansel Adams?" Avery asked.

"No, the ghost," Maeve said, pointing at the figure in the picture.

"This guy is your ghost?" Lissie asked, peering intently at the photograph in her hand.

"Well, he looked a little older last night. Okay, a LOT older. But the eyes are the same. I'll never forget those piercing eyes! He seemed so real! And totally creepy."

Charlotte pulled out her notebook and quickly jotted down all the details she could remember about Maeve's ghost. With her job as feature writer for the Abigail Adams *Sentinel*, Charlotte was used to paying attention to the details. It was the mark of a good investigative reporter, her teacher, Ms. Rodriguez, had told her.

"Are we going to eat or what?" Avery asked, reaching for a cracker and smothering it with peanut butter.

"How about putting some Swedish Fish on that peanut butter?" Maeve suggested.

"Swedish Fish on peanut butter?" Avery rolled her eyes as if it was the most absurd thing she'd ever heard. "That's just plain weird, Maeve."

"Hey, the fish tasted good with the chocolate last night, didn't they?" Maeve reminded her.

"Don't say chocolate unless you can back it up with the real thing!" Charlotte warned. "I have a major craving. That Hershey bar tasted so great last night."

"Here, Charlotte. Try a few Swedish Fish with that peanut-butter-cracker sandwich," Maeve said, passing a handful of the red fish toward Charlotte. "Trust me . . . I've got a feeling I'm on to something."

"You STILL have Swedish Fish left?" Charlotte asked. "How is that possible?"

"My motto is, 'Never leave home without a huge stash of fish from Irving's Toy and Card Shop,'" Maeve declared triumphantly.

Charlotte squished a couple of Swedish Fish into the bottom half of her peanut-butter-cracker sandwich, replaced the top cracker, and sank her teeth into the sweet treat. "Huh," Charlotte said. "This does taste good. But I'm not sure if it's actually good or if I'm just super hungry."

Maeve looked triumphant. "See? I was right. You know when people ask if you were stranded on a deserted island and you could only have one thing with you, what would it be? I bet you all would say you'd bring *moi*. Come on, admit it."

"Uh, Maeve?" Avery said. "You were freaking out about the mice. I don't think you'd be much help in the wilderness . . . even WITH your Swedish Fish. Besides," she added with a grin, "the bears would smell your perfume a mile away."

"Bears are beary, beary cute," Maeve cooed in response, grinning also.

"Look, girls!" Mr. Ramsey called from the window. "The wind calmed down—finally! And the clouds are thinning. I think the sun might actually shine today."

"Great! Can we go exploring?" Maeve asked. Even though she was tired, she was getting restless.

"But I thought you wanted to sleep," Charlotte pointed out.

"Sleep!? My Swedish Fish sugar rush just kicked in and I'm ready for anything!" Maeve jumped up and stretched.

"I don't see why we can't do a little exploring, but everyone will have to bundle up. It's still chilly out there."

As soon as the girls finished their peanut butter

breakfast, everyone piled on layers of warm clothing. Charlotte tied her dad's scarf over Maeve's hat so her ears and neck wouldn't freeze, and Lissie loaned Maeve a pair of warm boots.

"Hey, this wilderness mix 'n' match fashion look is starting to grow on me. It's kind of boho-chic or something. Katani should write about my look in her fashion tips for the next *Sentinel*," Maeve said, admiring her reflection in the window. "Oh . . . I miss Katani . . . and Isabel." The girls nodded in agreement as they put on their coats, gloves, and scarves.

"Everyone ready?" Mr. Ramsey asked when they were all suited up for the cold. He pushed the Hotel de Paris front door open, and a gust of wind immediately snatched at their hair and pushed them along the boardwalk.

Charlotte sucked in a breath of icy air. Even though it was cold, it made her feel fresh and alive. But it wasn't just the cold air. Charlotte thought she could feel the rugged spirit of the miners who had lived there decades earlier as she followed the others down the street.

"Cool! A saloon from the olden days," Avery called, darting inside an old building.

The others followed her, stopping just inside the door. The girls were quiet as they looked around at the empty barroom.

"Look at the wood," Lissie said, running her hand along the bar. "It's hand carved and beautiful."

"Looks like there used to be a mirror on that wall there," Mr. Ramsey pointed.

"It seems like the spirit of the Old West is still in this place . . . all around us," Lissie observed.

"Yeah, I can just imagine the cowboys swinging open those doors and stopping by here on their way back from the ranch," Charlotte mused, looking around the empty room that was still somehow full of life.

The girls shuffled out the door to continue exploring. Charlotte scanned the storefronts and buildings up and down Main Street. Everywhere there were reminders that this had once been a bustling, ordinary town full of ordinary places: a barbershop, a bakery, a dry goods store, and a blacksmith shop. At the end of the block was a tiny church with dark wood pews and beautiful stained glass windows.

"Did you know that many ghost towns have been ruined by vandals?" Lissie said. "We're lucky that Dry Gulch wasn't one of them. Most of the damage here seems to be from the wear and tear of the weather. Who would ever destroy such a piece of history on *purpose*?"

Charlotte had read up about Montana ghost towns before the trip, but Lissie had taken over the history lesson, offering up detail after detail about the town and life on the frontier. Charlotte found herself annoyed at Lissie's comments and even more irritated that her father seemed to hang on Lissie's every word. It was just frustrating to have one person dominate the whole conversation and think everything she said was so important.

"Imagine what it would be like to go to basket socials and calico balls," Lissie pondered.

"What are those?" Maeve asked.

"Socials and balls were the ways people used to meet boyfriends and girlfriends back in the day," Lissie said. "If you ask me, it sounds like it'd be a lot of fun."

"I didn't ask you," Charlotte muttered under her breath. She wished she wasn't so bothered by Lissie, but she just couldn't help how she felt. Lissie was just so frustratingly enthusiastic.

"I remember reading that there used to be a long chute that ran from the mine into town. In the winter, the locals had fun flying down the chute with frying pans," Lissie was saying.

"Cool! Where is that chute? I wanna try!" Avery exclaimed, looking around.

"Sorry, Ave. I think the chute was destroyed in the explosion," Charlotte informed her.

"Explosion?" Avery asked.

"Yeah, that's how Dry Gulch became a ghost town," Charlotte explained. "There was a mining accident, an explosion that killed a lot of people and closed the mine for good. It happened in 1944. The place was in rough shape then, anyway. Way past the glory days of the 1890s."

Maeve suddenly stopped dead in her tracks.

"What is it?" a curious Charlotte asked, following Maeve's gaze upward.

"I thought I saw lights flickering in that old building across the street," Maeve said.

"Time to chill, Maeve. The ghost was a dream. D-R-E-A-M," Avery mouthed.

"No, look over there." Maeve pointed. "Wilson's Boarding House."

"I see it too!" Charlotte shouted excitedly.

"Where? Where?!" Avery demanded.

"In the second window, right?" Maeve asked Charlotte, who nodded.

"Oh, I see them too!" a suddenly excited Avery blurted out. "It's going from the second window to the first window. There. There!"

The group scrambled around a huge snowdrift in the middle of Main Street and raced to the door of the boarding house.

"Hello. Hello?" Mr. Ramsey called into the darkness beyond the open door. He shushed the girls as he listened for a response. "Anyone there?" he called out again.

"I'm sure I saw a light!" Avery insisted. "Maybe it's on a timer or something."

"This town has never been wired for electricity," Mr. Ramsey said. "The only way there could be a light is if a person had a flashlight or a lantern, but there doesn't seem to be anyone around. I think with all this ghost talk we're letting our imaginations get the better of us."

"I don't know, Dad." Charlotte shook her head. "It's not like we were walking around looking for a ghost."

"Well, we better leave it for now," Mr. Ramsey said. "No one's going in there to investigate—it's too dangerous. The stairs look like they're rotting away."

Jail Time

"I want to check out the jail we saw yesterday," Avery said, sprinting down the street with Charlotte and Maeve close on her heels. "Come on! It's this way!"

Suddenly the jailhouse door swung open right in front of them. Avery screeched to a halt so fast she almost lost her balance.

Charlotte gulped and Maeve let out a shriek.

"Cool," Avery shouted. "Let's go in!"

"But why did *this* door randomly blow open?" Maeve asked. "I didn't feel a gust of wind or anything."

Avery ignored her and zipped into the jail.

"Hey! Get in here!" she shouted. "Guys, you gotta see this place!"

Charlotte felt the temperature drop ten degrees the moment she crossed over the threshold into the small jail. The walls were made of stone and the windows were tiny slits. Two imposing cells stood in front of them, complete with thick iron bars that ran from floor to ceiling. The air was chilly, dank, and damp. "It's creepy in here," Charlotte whispered to no one in particular. Maybe the ghosts of the jail were about to materialize. She felt the hairs on her arm begin to prickle. Dry Gulch was getting spooky.

"What a cool photo op. Come on, you two, get in there," Maeve said, ushering Charlotte and Avery into one of the jail cells. "Now try to look tough and lonely like real jailbirds," Maeve motioned as she backed away, trying to fit the whole cell into her viewfinder.

"Close the door, Avery. That'll make it look real!" Maeve said, gesturing for Avery to shut the cell door.

"NO!" Lissie yelled as Avery pulled hard at the door.

The sound of metal-on-metal reverberated in the small stone jail as the door clanged shut.

"What! What is it?!" Mr. Ramsey asked, rushing into

the jail, clearly alarmed by Lissie's scream. "Is everyone all right there?"

"I'm fine, but they're in a bit of trouble," Lissie motioned toward Avery and Charlotte, who were trapped inside the cell.

The two had such melancholy expressions on their faces that Mr. Ramsey couldn't help but laugh.

"It's NOT funny," Charlotte said with desperation, rattling at the iron bars.

"This is perfect! PERFECT!" Maeve proclaimed, snapping pictures from every angle.

"It's NOT perfect, Maeve," Charlotte cried, her voice rising. "How are we supposed to get out of here?"

"Well, in the movies there's usually a big ring of keys hanging on a hook somewhere. Hmmm. I found a hook, but no keys," Lissie said, scanning the walls.

"Could you two just grab the bars and give me your best sad look?" Maeve asked. "Closer together. Put your heads together. Now act like you'll never get out of there."

"Not funny, Maeve," Avery groaned. "It might be true."

"What if we never escape," Charlotte added, sinking to the floor and leaning her head against the wall. As brave as she was, Charlotte did not like small, closed spaces.

"Maybe the keys are in here somewhere," Lissie suggested as she and Mr. Ramsey frantically opened the desk drawers.

"Don't fear, my little jailbirds," Mr. Ramsey said in his fake French accent, attempting to lighten the mood. "Vee will bring you blankets to keep you warm."

"And I will bring you beans," Maeve crossed her heart. "Promise."

"Look at these wanted posters!" Lissie pulled the posters out of the drawer and handed them to Maeve.

"Hey, guys, it could be worse. You could be in the cell with Bad Bart here or Lester Grinch," Maeve said, showing the girls the yellowed wanted posters. "EWWWW! Those guys look like they wouldn't smell too good either."

"Come on, guys. This is soooo not funny anymore," Charlotte groaned.

"It wasn't funny to begin with. DO something! I don't want to spend the rest of my life locked up in this place," Avery pouted. "And Maeve. STOP IT with the pictures!"

"Okay," Maeve said. "But just one more!" The flash lit up the dark cell one last time.

"Wait a minute . . . look at this." Lissie held up a wooden box.

"It's just a box," Mr. Ramsey said.

"But listen to this," Lissie shook the box. "Maybe there are keys inside."

"So, open it already!" Avery shouted.

"It's locked," Lissie said, fiddling with the lock.

"You're kidding me." Avery sounded exasperated. "Now we have to find the key for the box that MIGHT have the keys to the cell? We are NEVER getting out of here!"

"Be right back." Mr. Ramsey darted out the door.

"Dad, don't leave me here!" a shaking Charlotte called after him.

"Silence, prisoners," Maeve said in a stern warden tone. "It's exercise time. Ready, march!"

"March where?" Avery asked.

"In a circle, of course," Maeve said, trying to look as tough as she sounded.

"In a circle?" Charlotte looked skeptical.

"Attention, soldiers. A-TEN-SHUN!" Maeve bellowed.

"Soldiers?" Avery asked quizzically. "I thought we were prisoners."

"Okay, whatever. A-TEN-SHUN, prisoners!" Maeve shouted again.

"Found it!" Mr. Ramsey cried as he came back into the jail.

"You found the keys?" Maeve asked.

"No, a crowbar," Mr. Ramsey said, brandishing the tool in front of him. "Let's get that box open and break you two outta jail!"

Sure enough, they found a rusty ring of keys in the box. A trembling Charlotte was relieved beyond belief when the iron-barred door creaked open and she could escape from beyond the dark, dank stone cell. Charlotte promised herself that she would never ever get into trouble because she never ever wanted to be in a jail cell again. Not even for fun!

"Okay, girls. Now that the jailbird crisis is over, maybe you'll realize that you have to be careful around here! Watch where you walk, stay together, and DON'T get locked in anywhere," Mr. Ramsey warned them. "This town is old and rickety and you can't mess around or somebody might get hurt."

His words fell on deaf ears as Avery and Charlotte, like true jailbirds, flew the coop and went sliding down the big snowdrift in the middle of the street.

"Jailbreak! Jailbreak!" Maeve called, rushing after them. "Criminals at large! Criminals at large!"

Charlotte locked eyes with Avery and they both nodded in silent agreement.

"Let's do it," Avery determined. The two girls rushed forward, each grabbing one of Maeve's arms. They hustled Maeve down the street and tossed her into a snow bank.

"Quick! Where's the camera?" Charlotte asked. "Say cheese, Maeve!"

Maeve stuck out her tongue, shaking the snow out of her curls.

Avery broke into uncontrollable giggles. "Wait!" she gasped, trying to catch her breath. "I have the perfect caption: 'Abominable Snowgirl Terrorizes Ghost Town!'"

Lissie helped Maeve to her feet and the whole group laughed all the way down the street to the General Store.

"Look!" Lissie exclaimed, pointing out the dates on the newspapers strewn behind the counter. The newspapers were yellowed and faded, but still readable.

"Whoa!" Charlotte exclaimed. "1944?! Right before the end of World War II. These newspapers are ancient!"

"Good," Avery said, gathering up a stack. "Old news. We can use them to help start a fire."

"Are you crazy?!" Charlotte shouted, snatching the stack of papers out of Avery's hand. "We can't burn these.

They're history. Plus, now I have something to read!"
Charlotte said, gazing lovingly at the delicate newspapers
in her hands.

"I agree, Charlotte. I was a history major in college.
Sometimes I think I'm more interested in the lives of people
in the past than I am of people I meet in my day-to-day life,"
Lissie said.

Charlotte wasn't impressed. She knew that Lissie was
just making conversation or whatever, but for some reason
it didn't feel that way. It seemed like Lissie was trying to
show off or something.

"Look over there," Avery said when they ventured out
into the street again. "It looks like an old tavern or something. I have me a hankerin' for a steak dinner," she said
in her best western drawl. Avery pushed through the one
swinging half-door that was still intact. The other side was
hanging by one rusty hinge. The moment Avery entered
the musty tavern, brandishing Mr. Ramsey's flashlight,
eerie music started playing.

Startled, Avery jumped back and crashed into the
swinging door, which clattered to the ground. She stum-
bled backward across the boardwalk and catapulted into a
soft snowdrift. All that could be seen of Avery was her feet
sticking up out of the snow.

Charlotte couldn't help cracking up.

"Don't laugh!" Avery commanded as she crawled out
of the snowdrift and brushed herself off. "That freaked me
out! What WAS that? Is there someone in there?"

"It's just a player piano," Maeve reported from the
door as she peeked into the darkness.

"But what made it start randomly playing like that?" Avery asked.

No one said anything, but they all had the same thought. Maybe Maeve really had seen a ghost.

"Hey, guys! Come here!" Lissie called. She was standing at the other end of the boardwalk. "I was fiddling with my cell phone and I actually got a bar of service! One little bar, but I might be able to make a call," Lissie said optimistically as she pushed some buttons. "Luckily, I programmed in the number to Big Sky Resort before I left. Wait! It's ringing!"

Lissie handed the phone to Mr. Ramsey. "Here," she said. "You need to check on the girls."

"Hello, this is Richard Ramsey. I was supposed to check into the resort yesterday. Some of my party should have arrived already: Isabel Martinez and Katani Summers?"

He glanced at Charlotte, Maeve, and Avery, who were staring up at him with expectant eyes. Mr. Ramsey nodded to let them know that Katani and Isabel had arrived safely.

"Our rental vehicle broke down on the way to the resort. We're safe, but we are stuck in . . . Hello? Hello?"

"Lost the connection?" Lissie asked.

Mr. Ramsey nodded his head slowly and looked at the girls' disappointed faces. "Don't worry. At least we know that Katani and Isabel are safe. And I'm almost positive the Big Sky people were on the line long enough to hear that we're safe, too," Mr. Ramsey reassured them.

"I'm sure the resort is taking good care of your friends," Lissie told the girls.

The girls trudged glumly back toward the hotel.

"I bet those guys are having a blast," Avery said in a downtrodden voice.

"Do you think they're hanging out with Nik and Sam?" Charlotte wondered.

"Nik and Sam!" Maeve groaned and threw up her arms dramatically. "I can't believe I'm stuck in a ghost town while Nik and Sam are only like an hour away. It so figures!"

"If I were them, I'd be relaxing in that gigantic hot tub from the brochure right now," Charlotte said.

"How great would it be to slip into the hot bubbly water? I can almost feel it now." Maeve daydreamed with her eyes shut, imagining every bubble.

"I wish I could feel it now," Avery said as they opened the door to the cold, dry hotel. Mr. Ramsey began poking at the fire to stir it back to life.

14

Kgirl to the Rescue

I'll meet you in the Missouri ballroom in about five minutes then, okay?" Nik and Sam's mom smiled. "There should be a security guard at the door. Just show him this pass and he'll let you in right away. If he gives you any trouble, tell him to call me."

"Okay," Isabel said, taking the pass from her hand. "I'm so excited!" she squealed, turning to Katani as soon as the door to their suite was closed. "I've never been to a real live concert rehearsal before."

"Me neither," Katani said with a grin. "This is just plain *awesome*."

The girls stopped at the front desk on the way to the theater to see if there was any word from Mr. Ramsey and the rest of the BSG. The front desk clerk informed them that Mr. Ramsey had called and said their rental car had broken down.

"Broken down?" Katani asked. They had been hoping that Mr. Ramsey and the girls had stopped at a hotel or rest stop to wait out the storm. This sounded more serious. "Where *are* they?"

"That's the problem," the clerk told her. "The phone went dead before we could get a location from them."

"Dead?" Katani repeated ominously.

"Mr. Ramsey said they were safe," the clerk assured the girls.

"But where are they?" Isabel wondered aloud.

"The state police have been notified. There's a small search party out looking for them now."

"A search party?" Isabel asked as concern welled up inside of her.

The clerk patted Isabel comfortingly on the shoulder. "Don't worry, sweetie! I'm sure they're fine. No need to be concerned. They've obviously found shelter, and they'll be rescued when the roads are clear. Now, what are you girls doing this morning?"

"We're going to watch Nik and Sam's concert rehearsal," Katani told her.

"That sounds like great fun. Have a good time and try not to worry about your friends. Do you need anything?" the clerk asked warmly.

"No, thank you," Katani said, standing up straight and tall. "We'll be fine . . . right, Isabel?"

Isabel nodded. She just crossed her fingers and hoped with all her might that the others were fine, too.

Just as they turned away from the front desk, Katani's cell phone rang. She checked the caller ID and flipped it open to talk to her mother.

"How are things in the Wild Wild West?" Mrs. Summers asked in a cheery tone.

"Uh, fine," Katani answered. She wasn't sure how to inform her mother that things were anything but fine.

"What's wrong, sweetie?" Mrs. Summers immediately sensed that something was amiss.

"Nothing is wrong. I mean, *I'm* fine," Katani stammered. Hearing her mother's voice made tears spring to Katani's eyes. She took a deep breath.

"Mr. Ramsey called and told you I'd be riding to the resort with Nik and Sam, right?"

"Yes. You're okay, Katani, aren't you?" Mrs. Summers asked, sounding very concerned.

"Well, Isabel and I are fine. We're at Big Sky with Nik and Sam. But there was a huge snowstorm—a blizzard, really—and Mr. Ramsey and the other girls are . . ."

"Are what?"

"They're missing. They never made it to the resort last night," Katani told her mother. "We just heard from the front desk that they're safe, but stuck somewhere."

"So you're there ALONE?" Mrs. Summers asked.

"No. Nik and Sam's parents are here and they're making sure we're okay. We had a sleepover in their suite last night and now we're going to watch their rehearsal."

"You and Isabel stick together, Katani. Make sure to keep me posted," Mrs. Summers said.

"I will, Mom. We'll be okay . . . really. Talk to you later." Katani flipped the phone shut. "All right," she said, turning to Isabel. "Let's go." She wondered if Avery and Maeve's parents knew they were missing.

Music and Makeovers

Isabel and Katani could hear the music through the doors of the Missouri Ballroom. The security guard opened the door when he saw them as if he were expecting them . . . almost as if they were VIPs!

The twins were in the middle of "Every Little Step," a nice, slow ballad that Nik was belting out in her sweet, sad voice. Their dad was playing an acoustic bass. "Hold up! Hold on a second!" he called.

"The drum part isn't quite right," he explained. "You girls want to take a break while we work this out?"

Nik and Sam jumped down from the stage and made a beeline for Isabel and Katani.

"Hey, Katani, Iz! Thanks for coming," Sam said. "We need to decide what to wear to the concert!"

"Let Katani help," Isabel offered.

"Really?" Nik asked as she turned toward Katani. The twins had commented to each other how fashionable Katani always looked. "You'd do that?"

"We were *hoping* we could get some free advice from a future famous designer," Sam said with a twinkle in her eye.

"Don't worry, girls. I'm on it," Katani said. "What's my budget?"

"Our dad usually says, 'Just don't break the bank,'" Nik said.

As soon as the girls returned to the stage, Katani and

Isabel dashed off to the resort boutique. They were on a fashion mission.

Katani surveyed the store and finally picked up two cropped equestrian jackets in midnight blue velvet and two silky white shirts to go underneath.

"Perfect," Isabel said with approval. "Nice job, Kgirl."

Excited about their purchases, they ran back to the greenroom to show Nik and Sam.

The twins were just taking another break from their rehearsal as Katani and Isabel returned.

"Check it out. I think this look is perfect for you. The equestrian jackets are western and romantic at the same time. And these shirts are just right—they'll even shimmer a little under the lights. Try everything on, and then I'll show you the final touch," Katani urged.

"These jackets are *amazing*," Nik said, twirling around.

"How did you know they would fit?" Sam wondered.

"Please, I'm a professional," Katani said, rolling her eyes with a casual shrug.

"So what's the last touch?" Nik asked.

"Ta-da!" Katani announced, holding up two of her colorful scarves. "The outfits are great, but they need a dash of color to take them to the next level. Here's a lime green scarf for you, Sam, and a purple one for you, Nik. Wear them as low-slung belts on your jeans. Here, Isabel, help me thread them through the loops." Katani tied the scarves expertly for the twins and stood back to admire her fashion makeovers.

"How did you know these are our favorite colors?" Sam wondered.

"Last night you said that your bedroom was lime green, Sam, and Nik told me she loved everything purple. Remember?" Katani asked.

"Girls!" Nik and Sam's mom called from the stage.

"Wait till they see us!" Nik squealed.

"Katani, you're a miracle worker!" Sam gave Katani an exuberant hug.

"Break a leg," Katani called after the twins as they dashed back onstage.

Katani and Isabel watched the rest of the rehearsal from the wings.

"Oh, I *love* this song!" Isabel exclaimed as they started their last number, "Every Little Step." "It makes me think of my dad."

Isabel started singing the lyrics softly from the wing. "There's a little girl with a barrette in her hair bouncing on daddy's knee . . ."

Sam saw Isabel singing along and motioned for her to join them onstage.

Isabel shook her head no, but Katani gave her a little shove, and she reluctantly walked out into the lights.

Once she was up there, Isabel inched over to center stage. "Here, you can share my microphone," Sam said as she pulled Isabel closer.

The twins continued singing. Isabel started to join in softly, but eventually she lost her self-consciousness and really let it out. She was singing with all her might. "Daddy asked his little girl to dance with him one last time . . ." Isabel couldn't believe how good it felt to let go and sing her heart out.

A Fine Stew

"I'm beginning to wish I never heard the word 'adventure,'" Maeve complained as the stranded group tried to decide what they were going to eat for dinner, huddled around the fireplace at the Hotel de Paris. "Beans were an adventure last night, but tonight they're BORING!"

"At least we have something to eat," Lissie pointed out. "If the Mountain Rover had broken down ten miles up the road, we'd be very hungry by now. I think we'd be getting by on Swedish Fish and trail mix."

"Lissie's right. We're lucky to have a roof over our heads, a fire to keep us warm, and something to put in our stomachs, even if it's just beans," Mr. Ramsey said.

"How far from town did you walk this afternoon, Dad?" Charlotte asked. Mr. Ramsey had gone on an expedition to see if there was any sign of a rescue team.

"Not far," Mr. Ramsey admitted. "At the edge of town the drifts were so high! Over my head, even. I have no idea how long it will take them to clear the road and discover the Mountain Rover."

"Don't worry," Lissie said, patting Mr. Ramsey's back. "Montana is used to this kind of weather. They have to clear the highways first. And they know we're missing now. I'm sure that someone—the state police, probably—has a search party out looking for us. We'll be rescued before we know it."

Mr. Ramsey didn't say anything but smiled gratefully at Lissie. He was getting a little tired of their ghost town adventure as well.

Charlotte picked up the poker and pushed around

the logs on the fire. The flames crackled and hissed at her. Charlotte couldn't even look at Maeve and Avery. The girls had been making faces at each other since yesterday. She knew they were convinced that her father had a crush on Lissie. Charlotte poked at a big log, which rolled over the top of a smaller log and broke it with a loud crack. The embers glowed and winked beneath the log.

Well, they're wrong, Charlotte thought. Dad is just tired and worried. That's all. He's not interested in Lissie. She just isn't his type. Charlotte wasn't sure what type was her father's, but she knew it was definitely not Lissie.

"I can't believe it! It's dark already," Avery said, looking out the window. "It's like we didn't have a real day at all."

The afternoon had turned dark and dreary and even though it was only four in the afternoon, it seemed like it was midnight.

"This place is really creepy." Maeve shivered.

"I think it's cool," Charlotte countered. "Dry Gulch is like this abandoned piece of history."

"Come on, Char, get real. This town doesn't seem all that abandoned," Avery said.

"We saw those flickering lights in the boardinghouse," Maeve reminded Charlotte.

"And don't forget that piano," Avery added. "It just randomly started playing."

"That was a player piano, Avery," Charlotte said. "It's supposed to play music like that."

"Yeah, but they usually don't start and stop all by themselves," Avery pointed out.

"Doors opening . . ." Maeve said ominously.

"And slamming shut," Avery continued.

"And don't forget getting locked in the jail cell!" Maeve cried.

"How could I forget? You took enough pictures to fill up a whole photo album!" Charlotte exclaimed.

"Yeah, I did," Maeve giggled to herself. "I can't wait to see how they turn out."

"Maeve's right, Char!" Avery said. "This place is creepy. It's almost as if someone is trying to scare us off."

"There IS someone trying to scare us off," Maeve asserted confidently.

"Who?" Charlotte asked.

"Hello! Charlotte, I told you about the ghost."

Charlotte gave Maeve a skeptical look.

"Charlotte, there IS a ghost in this town and I SAW him," Maeve insisted.

"Yes, you did," said a grave voice.

The girls screamed and huddled together.

Mr. Ramsey grabbed the poker and jumped up.

Slow, steady footsteps moved across the floor from the back of the room. Out of the darkness, a looming figure appeared and stood behind the couch. The figure was a tall, grizzled old man in a cowboy hat. Maeve's eyes widened as she realized that the ghost from the night before was standing right before their very eyes.

Tonight, instead of the long coat, he was wearing a wide, green poncho. He was also carrying a rifle, which he held across his chest, the long black muzzle pointing toward the ceiling.

"It's Maeve's ghost!" Avery gasped.

"Just as you described him," Charlotte murmured.

"I told you it was true. I told you!" Maeve cried.

The ghost put up a hand in a calming gesture, letting the rifle hang loosely at his side. "I mean you no trouble," the man said in a deep, gravelly voice.

"Then put the rifle down," Mr. Ramsey commanded, adjusting his grip on the poker.

The old man nodded and leaned down to place the rifle on the floor. "It ain't loaded right now, anyhow," he said.

"I have heard that before," Mr. Ramsey said dryly. For a moment the air was silent but heavy with expectation. Charlotte couldn't breathe. Had she finally gotten her wish? Was she really and truly seeing a ghost?

"Didn't mean to scare you none," the man repeated. "Ain't used to visitors, is all. Most people don't bother to stop in Dry Gulch anymore."

"You mean you *live* here?" Lissie asked tentatively.

The man nodded. "Lived here since I came back from the war. The Second World War, that is. Lived here before the war, too. But when I came back in forty-five, Dry Gulch was deserted. Pretty much like it is today. Everyone left after the mining accident of forty-four."

"Please, sir," Mr. Ramsey gestured. "Have a seat by the fire and warm up."

The old man moved from behind the couch and sat down in the wingback chair by the fire. Charlotte couldn't help but draw back as he walked toward the BSG huddle. Despite his insistence that he wasn't there to cause any harm, there was something menacing about his appearance. And it didn't help that a scowl seemed to be permanently etched on his face.

Once he sat down, the group let out a collective sigh of relief. Sitting there in the chair, the old cowboy looked more like a real person and less like a ghostly apparition.

It was quiet for a long while, with only the crackling fire filling in the silence.

"Why do you stay in this abandoned place all by yourself?" Mr. Ramsey finally asked.

"I got my reasons," the gruff man replied.

"Were you the one slamming doors and blinking lights and starting the player piano?" Lissie asked, sitting forward in her chair to face the old man on the other side of the fireplace.

The man didn't reply but instead stared across at Lissie, apparently fascinated by her appearance.

"We're obviously stranded, and to purposely scare us, especially when we have young girls in our group, is just . . . just plain MEAN," Lissie scolded.

The man did not respond but continued to stare intently at Lissie.

"What are you looking at?" Lissie demanded as she sat back in her seat.

The man dropped his eyes to the floor. "Sorry, miss," he grumbled. "Ain't used to bein' around folks. Suppose I lost my manners."

"Well, maybe we should start with introductions, then. I'm Lissie. What's your name?"

When the man looked up again, his glare had softened,

but he still observed Lissie as if she had two heads. He didn't say anything for a while and Charlotte wondered if he had forgotten his name altogether.

"JT will do just fine," he finally responded. Then, in an old-fashioned, courtly way, JT doffed his hat to Lissie and the girls.

Maeve broke away from the huddle and dropped into a curtsy. "Pleased to meet you, JT," she quipped.

Charlotte couldn't help giggling. Maeve had probably picked up her etiquette skills from some old movie about Queen Victoria.

Mr. Ramsey finally released his death grip on the poker. "I'm Richard Ramsey," he said to JT. "Sorry about the poker. You gave us quite a shock."

"No bother. You folks must be hungry. I got an old kerosene stove stashed in the summer kitchen out back," JT told them. "In fact, I rustled myself up some beef stew before the blizzard the other night. Like to keep the non-canned food out back so as not to attract any critters into the hotel here."

Critters, Maeve mouthed to Avery, who couldn't help smiling. Avery loved "critters."

JT got up and gestured for them to follow. He led them through the kitchen and into the servant wing of the hotel. They hadn't ventured into this area yet, and everyone was surprised to find it quite homey.

"I moved my things—everything that wasn't destroyed in the blast, that is—here," JT explained.

"The blast?" Avery asked.

"The mining explosion. My house was back there on

Cedar Street and almost everything was destroyed."

JT gazed out the window. "Dry Gulch was a real nice town before the disaster," he reflected. "But when I came back from Germany at the end of the war, it was deserted. Everyone was gone."

"Why did you stay, then?" Lissie asked.

JT looked as if he was the one who'd seen a ghost. Charlotte wasn't sure if he had even heard the question, but finally he said, "I was waiting."

The answer sent shivers up and down Charlotte's spine.

JT turned away and took up a flint to light the kerosene stove. From the ancient icebox, he removed a large pot.

"Beef stew," Avery mouthed to Charlotte. She motioned for Maeve and Charlotte to lean in. "I don't care if this guy is a ghost . . . we're gonna get to eat REAL food!" she whispered.

"You're welcome to share when the stew heats up," JT said, breaking down the partially frozen block of stew with a big, wooden spoon. "It's nothin' fancy, but it'll do."

"Thank you," Mr. Ramsey said. "The girls are very hungry, and a hot meal in our stomachs would certainly keep us warm this evening and cheer us up. We're all a little disappointed to be missing out on some of our trip."

JT nodded at Mr. Ramsey and then his eyes settled again on Lissie.

The group decided to eat in front of the fire in the main part of the hotel. Charlotte, Avery, and Maeve gathered bowls and silverware as JT grabbed the stew pot with a big potholder and disappeared through the service entrance of the hotel.

The smell of the stew was wonderful—rich and beefy and peppered with pungent herbs. Charlotte's stomach growled as JT ladled the stew into bowls and gestured for Lissie to pass them to the girls. Charlotte was happy to find that besides tender pieces of beef in a rich gravylike broth, the stew had chunks of onions, tomatoes, potatoes, and carrots.

The group was silent as they devoured the rich, savory stew, their first hot meal in what seemed like forever. Charlotte couldn't help notice that between bites, JT was still observing Lissie very intently. What was that all about? *Maybe JT's fascinated with Lissie's eyes or something*, Charlotte thought. They were kind of a strange color—a bright yellow-brown—like a cat's eyes, almost. Charlotte's father had mentioned their unique color when they first met Lissie at the airport. Charlotte didn't care for the color . . . not one bit.

Finally, Maeve broke the silence. "Mr. . . . JT, were you ever married?

Charlotte stiffened. What was Maeve thinking? It was pretty rude to ask someone she barely knew such a personal question. Charlotte's eyes shifted quickly to the old man's face. Was he offended? It was hard to tell. JT didn't look up. He didn't even break the regular rhythm of his spoon moving from bowl to mouth. Charlotte was starting to think he hadn't even heard Maeve's question when he suddenly dropped the spoon into his bowl.

"Might have been," he muttered, not even looking up.

"You mean you're not sure if you were married?" Maeve asked. Charlotte tapped her on the arm and made a "cut it out" sign.

JT didn't seem to notice. "It was so long ago, I sometimes wonder if it was all a dream," he mused before picking up his spoon again.

Avery looked at Charlotte and rolled her eyes. Maeve looked like she was hoping with all her might JT would go on. After a minute of silence, Avery spoke up.

"We keep hearing these howling noises," she said. Now that they knew it was probably not a ghost, she was curious to identify the mysterious sounds. "Do you know what it could be?" she asked JT.

JT looked up from his stew and scowled. "Don't pay no nevermind to that howling," he said before slurping another bite. "It's the Wild West . . . what do you expect?"

Avery was shocked at his reaction. Maeve could pry into his personal life, but she couldn't ask a normal question about howling?! This guy was definitely *weird*.

"I'll leave you now," JT said as soon as his bowl was empty. "G'night." And with that he disappeared into the darkness at the back of the hotel.

The group was silent. Charlotte was wondering if, like her, everyone else was afraid to say anything in case JT was listening in. Finally, she worked up the nerve to lean over and whisper in her father's ear. "Do you think he's crazy, Dad?" she asked.

Mr. Ramsey shook his head. "No, I think that he's just an old and very lonely man. Imagine living alone here in this desolate place for over sixty years."

Charlotte nodded. "Did you notice how he kept staring at Lissie?" she asked in a low voice. "Why do you think he did that?"

Mr. Ramsey shrugged again. "I'm not sure. Lissie's eyes are kind of an interesting color."

Charlotte's heart skipped a beat. She was annoyed that her father mentioned Lissie's eyes. She couldn't help wondering . . . were Avery and Maeve right? Did her father actually have a crush on Lissie?

There were no animal charades that night. Perhaps it was because they were all comfortably full from stew or maybe it was the long day of exploring, but everyone was exhausted and fell asleep pretty much as soon as their heads hit their pillows.

Later, in the middle of the night, they were all startled awake by loud howls.

"What IS that?" Maeve asked.

"Not a ghost," Avery said.

"Could it be a coyote?" Charlotte asked.

"It doesn't really sound like a coyote or a wolf," Avery put her hand to her ear to listen harder.

"Maybe it's a mountain lion," Lissie suggested.

Maeve covered her head with her blanket and scrunched into a ball. "Lions and tigers and bears . . . Get me out of this place!"

15

Grommet Girls

S o what's the BSG plan for today?" Nik asked, as she sipped her hot chocolate.

Sam, Nik, Katani, and Isabel had ordered room service and were just finishing a scrumptious breakfast in front of the roaring fire.

"Whatever we do, it should be outside!" Isabel said. "It's gorgeous out there. The snow's so fluffy! Do you guys ski?" she asked.

"We haven't ever," Sam replied. "But we're up for anything. We love to try new things."

"There's tons to do at this place," Katani, who'd been looking at the resort's activity brochure, reported. She tossed the pamphlet to Nik.

"Wow! You name it, they got it! Skiing, snowboarding, ice-skating, dogsledding, snowshoeing, snowmobiling, et cetera, et cetera," Nik read off.

"Everything sounds pretty athletic to me," Katani said. "I'm not too good at sports. I'd love to go for a sleigh ride, though. Look! It even says they hand out hot chocolate and blankets."

"That sounds nice . . . all warm and cozy," Sam said.

"And safe from embarrassing sports bloopers," Katani added, nodding in agreement.

"But don't you want to get out there and run around?" Nik pleaded, looking longingly at the brochure.

In the end the girls just decided to bundle up and go exploring. With no real plan in mind, they ventured off into Big Sky Resort's winter wonderland.

"Look, there's the dogsled kennel," Nik pointed out.

"Avery would love this," Katani said with a laugh. "Maybe when they get here she'll go mushing!"

"IF they ever get here," Isabel said softly.

Katani's face fell and she leaned over to give Isabel a quick hug. "I'm scared too, Iz. But they called and said they were okay. Maybe they'll be waiting for us in the suite when we get back."

Isabel smiled weakly. "Maybe you're right. I hope so."

Katani grabbed her sensitive friend's hand and gave it a reassuring squeeze.

"Those dogs are so cute!" Nik cooed.

"Avery will totally flip. She's such a dog person," Katani informed them.

"We are, too!" Sam exclaimed. "We have three."

"Three dogs, five horses, six cats, four ducks, three guineas, and one hamster," Nik rattled off.

"Maeve has guinea pigs, too!" Isabel said. "They're so adorable and sweet."

"Those dogs must be ten times the size of Marty,"

Katani exclaimed. She reached into her pocket and her hand closed over one of Marty's dog biscuits.

"Hi, girls," one of the resort employees, who was hitching up the dogs, greeted them. "Pretty impressive dogs, aren't they? They're Siberian huskies."

One of the dogs barked and Katani jumped back.

"Don't worry, the dogs are very friendly. They have gentle spirits, despite the barking. Is that a dog biscuit you have there? Go ahead and offer it to Juno—the lead dog— if you like. I promise he won't bite."

Katani hesitated for a moment and then held out the biscuit. Juno gazed at her with piercing blue eyes, sniffed the biscuit, and took it gently from her hand.

A group of school kids on a field trip tromped by in snowshoes. Suddenly, one of the girls shrieked, "No WAY, it's Nik and Sam! Look guys . . . NIK AND SAM!"

Nik and Sam shot worried looks at Katani and Isabel. Right now the twins just wanted to be regular kids.

Soon the whole crowd started buzzing. Kids were craning their necks to catch a peek of the twins. Katani could see the neat line starting to break up and the whole group coming toward them.

Katani leaned closer to her new friends. "Okay," she whispered. "Just smile and wave." Katani steered the twins away. "Now MOVE!"

The girls smiled and offered friendly waves as Katani steadily pushed them away from the fan craziness.

"No eye contact," Katani said firmly. "Don't look back and keep moving!"

The twins moved quickly away from the dogsledding

area and then speed-walked to the ski complex.

"Is anyone following us?" Sam asked.

Isabel glanced back. "No. We escaped."

"Thanks, girls!" Nik cried, clearly relieved.

"Yeah, I just wasn't in the mood for an autograph signing session," Sam agreed.

"Hey, wait up!" a voice rang out, and the four girls jumped, thinking the crowd had somehow caught up with them.

Katani whipped around and blushed when she saw Daniel and his posse.

Daniel looked fab with his bright blue and gray ski jumpsuit and goggles perched on his head.

"Where are your boards?" he asked. "I'll show you a run that'll knock your socks off."

"We haven't decided if we want to board yet. We're still exploring what's out here," Nik said.

"We might ski," Sam added.

"Skiing? No way! Boarding is where it's at! You get this awesome floating sensation when you hit a patch of *sick pow*."

"Huh?" Nik asked.

"*Sick pow* is great snow," Daniel explained. "Come on. You'll love shredding downhill and going airborne."

"Airborne?" Katani asked. She did *not* like the sound of that at all!

"Ask for Tronni at the snowboarding school. He'll set you up. He's the best instructor for *shreducation*. He'll get you started without looking like you're 'rolling down the windows,' " Daniel told them.

"Rolling down the windows?" Nik asked. Daniel sounded like he was speaking a foreign language.

"That's *snowcabulary* for waving your arms frantically as you're trying to get your balance," Daniel said, demonstrating the move himself.

"What are we getting ourselves into?" Sam whispered to Katani. "I just want to balance on my own two feet!"

"Maybe after a few lessons you'll be able to run with the pros," Daniel said with a wink as he headed off for the ski lift.

"That sounded like a challenge," Sam said.

"I'm up for it." Nik grinned, heading for the instructor's hut.

"Sounds like fun," Isabel agreed.

"Sounds like I'll be in a cast by the end of the day." Katani looked skeptical.

"Come on, Katani. You weren't sure about trying pool either and look how well that turned out," Isabel reminded her.

"But pool didn't involve flying down a mountain at top speed," Katani pointed out.

"Come on, you might be surprised and really like it!" Isabel encouraged her. "I'm sure we'll start off on a bunny hill or something."

Katani and Sam exchanged looks. "I'm only up for it if you are," Sam responded.

Katani took a deep breath. "All right," she slowly nodded her head. "I guess I'm in."

"Woohoo!" Isabel and Nik cheered. "Let's go."

Back inside the hotel they found Tronni, who started

off by getting them suited up for the adventure. Boards, boots, bindings, snow pants, helmets, goggles—the gear just kept coming. Katani wondered if they were actually going to the moon instead of just up a mountain.

Once they finally got outside, they discovered that Daniel was right about one thing—Tronni was a great instructor. He broke everything down into little parts that were easy to understand, and he was superpatient.

"Okay, my little snow bunnies," he smiled at them after they'd all learned how to strap into their boards. "We're going to start with a heelslide."

The group was standing at the little instruction area outside the snowboard hut where there was a tiny slope for first-timers to practice on.

"With your snowboard facing across the slope, stand up so you are looking down the slope. Make sure to keep your weight on your heels," Tronni stressed.

Katani wobbled a little and she wasn't even moving. *Please don't let me fall down before I even have a chance to get started*, Katani pleaded softly to herself.

"Not now, but when I tell you to, point your toes on both feet just a little bit, and you will start to slide down the hill. Pull back on your toes when you want to stop. Okay, now. Point your toes on both feet just a bit!" Tronni directed.

"Hey, Sleeping Beauty! Wanna join the rest of us at the bottom of the hill?" Tronni called after a few moments.

Startled, Katani realized she had closed her eyes out of fear and had barely moved at all. Everyone else was at the bottom of the practice run. Part of her wanted to stay right where she was at the top of the slope. She could probably unstrap the board and walk down to safety. But another part of her wanted to get past her fear and board down to the others. Could she do it without crashing into them?

Tronni took the tow rope back up to the top of the tiny slope and slowly coaxed Katani into action. "Okay, Katani, no fears," Tronni whispered in her ear. "You are going to glide down this hill looking like a pro. Stand straight and tall, and bend your knees slightly. Relax and think good thoughts. Now point your toes."

Without thinking, Katani did what she'd been told. She pointed her toes and started moving. Isabel, Nik, and Sam all cheered her on. "Way to go, Kgirl! You're doing it!"

Tronni was a miracle worker. He seemed to know just what Katani was thinking and how to talk her through her fears.

The whole group practiced the heelslide over and over again. Katani slowly got the feel for how to start and stop by either pushing down or pulling up her toes.

After they were comfortable with the heelslide, Tronni taught the girls the falling leaf pattern, which was a technique they would use most of the time. They would slowly slide back and forth—just like a falling leaf—as they descended the mountain. "Remember to stay on your heelside edge the entire time," Tronni reminded them. "Practice it till it comes naturally."

Later on Tronni taught the girls how to skate. "This is how you'll get across flat areas, like when you're going to the chairlift," Tronni told them. With their front feet firmly attached to the boards, they released their back feet from the straps and used them to propel themselves along the snow.

"See?" Isabel said, seeing that Katani was getting the hang of it. "It's not as hard as you thought, is it?"

Katani grinned. For the first time that morning she felt a burst of confidence.

"Okay, that's it! You guys are ready for the slopes. Remember to detach your back foot from the board when you're riding the lift. I'll take the first run with you."

They all followed Tronni and waited in line for the chairlift to take them up the slope.

Katani looked at Isabel as they neared the front of the lift line. "I can't believe we're doing this!" Katani said, looking around nervously.

"Oh my gosh!" Sam exclaimed. "My mind just went completely blank. I can't remember anything at all!"

"She always says that before she gets onstage," Nik confided. "Every time!"

"Relax, Sam," Isabel said in a soothing tone. "Remember Tronni said to skate over to the line and just sit down as the chair comes up behind us. This is supposed to be the easy part."

Isabel didn't have a chance to continue because it was time to skate to the lift. "Remember," she reminded Katani. "We're supposed to keep the board pointing forward until it lifts off the snow."

Katani nodded. She felt like she could hardly breathe. Where was the confidence she felt just a minute ago?

As the chair came around, they both sat down and pulled the safety bar into place.

"We did it! We're on!" Katani exclaimed, relieved that she had gotten that far. They were on the chairlift.

As the chairlift rose higher and higher, Katani felt her nervousness returning. She glanced back at Nik and Sam in the chair behind them. Nik gave her a thumbs up. Katani had a tight grip on the side of the chair and could only send a weak smile in return.

"Izzy, what have we gotten ourselves into?"

"Get ready, Katani. We're almost at the unloading spot."

"I don't want to get off! Can't we just ride back down again?" Katani pleaded.

Isabel couldn't help giggling. "I don't think they'll let us do that. Okay, here we go. Remember keep your board straight," she coached.

"Straight. Straight. Keep the board straight," Katani repeated as they approached the unloading area.

"And keep your nose up," Isabel added.

"My nose?" Katani touched her finger to her nose. *What does my nose have to do with anything?* she thought as her board touched the snow and she began to slide down the little hill toward the top of the slope.

"Nose up!" Isabel shouted.

Katani tilted her head and raised her nose into the air, which threw her completely off balance. Her arms wind-milled in the air as she tried to recover.

"Not the nose on your face, Katani! The *snowboard's* nose. Pull your toes up. Remember the heelslide. Just do what Tronni taught you," Isabel called to Katani.

Suddenly it clicked. Katani rocked back on her heel and put her back foot down, sliding to a stop.

"Hey!" Nik called out from behind her. "You did it!"

"Ahhhhhh!" Sam screamed. "Look out!"

Sam crashed into Nik, who toppled against Isabel, who shot forward and collided with Katani. Just as quickly as she'd gotten her balance, Katani lost it again and went down in a big pile of arms and legs.

"Good thing we're singers instead of snowboarders," Sam giggled.

The four hurried to untangle themselves before Tronni arrived on the scene.

"Perfect," Tronni nodded approvingly when he joined them at the top of the slope, unaware of their hilariously jumbled exit from the chairlift. "Look at you! A group of model students."

The four girls exchanged sly smiles.

"Everybody got their right foot back in the strap?" Tronni asked, looking around.

Katani secured her foot and straightened back up. Then she took a good look at the hill in front of them. This was supposed to be a beginner hill, but it seemed way too steep for that. But instead of freaking out again, Katani focused on what Tronni was saying.

"Remember the heelslide and the falling leaf pattern. You guys know what to do. Okay, goggles on! Let's do this!"

Nik and Sam pushed off at the same time, closely followed by Isabel.

"Okay, Katani, your turn," said Tronni.

Katani took a deep breath and pushed down with the toes of her right foot. She didn't want to go too fast, so she raised her toes often. Slowly but steadily, she made her way down the hill in the falling leaf pattern.

"Go, girls!" Katani heard someone shouting from behind her. She looked up to see Daniel and his group of buddies swishing down the hill, spraying snow in every direction. He gave Katani a big thumbs-up as he whizzed by and then turned back and shouted, "SHRED ON, GROMMETS!"

"Grommets? What's that supposed to mean?" Katani asked Tronni.

Tronni laughed. "Don't get your feathers ruffled, Katani. Grommet just means you're a beginner."

"Guess we can live with that," Nik said. "Come on! Let's catch up to those boys."

With that, the grommets made their way down the snowy slope.

CHAPTER

16

The Discovery

J T, that chili was delish," Maeve said as the old man poured
a kettle of boiling water into the dishpan. "For a ghost—
former ghost, I mean—you're a really awesome cook,"
she added as she gulped down another delicious spoonful.

"You all seemed to enjoy the stew I made, so I started
workin' on the chili first thing this morning. Should have
enough leftovers for supper iffin' you're still here this evening," JT mumbled as he scrubbed the empty chili pot.

"It's almost worth being stuck here for that chili!"
Maeve said as she patted her stomach.

Avery glared at Maeve. Ghost town or not, this was
JT's home, and it seemed kind of rude to make JT's home
seem like a horrible place—a place they were "stuck" in.

"That cornbread was the best I've ever had," Avery
chimed in. "How do you even bake it without an oven?"

"You city folk got a lot to learn about campfire cooking, don't you?" JT remarked, adding a little cold water to
the hot. "Where are the others?"

"Well, Charlotte's probably writing in her journal," Maeve surmised.

"Or reading those old newspapers," Avery suggested. "Whenever you can't find Charlotte, she's usually reading or writing."

"And the other two? Where'd they get to?" JT asked.

Avery and Maeve exchanged knowing looks.

"Maybe they went for a walk," Avery said.

"A long, *romantic* walk," Maeve added.

"What are you two girls getting at?" JT asked.

"We think there's a romance brewing between Mr. Ramsey and Lissie," Maeve informed him.

Charlotte arrived at the kitchen door just as the words came out of Maeve's mouth. It wasn't a big shock—she knew her friends thought there was something going on between her father and Lissie—but she instinctively took a step back to see what else they had to say.

"Ahhhh!" JT waved a hand at them. "You got bats flying around in your heads if you think that. Those two are just friends."

"How do you know?" Maeve asked.

"I just do, is all," JT said with a faraway look in his eyes. "I know romance when I see it."

Charlotte breathed in sharply. She agreed with JT— Maeve and Avery were being ridiculous! Her father was too busy with his writing to be interested in getting a girlfriend at all, much less a girlfriend with weird cat eyes.

"Can I help with cleanup, too?" Charlotte asked as she joined them.

"No need. Many hands make light work, and we're

about all finished here," JT said as he tossed the dish towel over his shoulder. "Maeve and Avery were telling me you're a buddin' writer. You like to read, too?"

"JT is getting very chatty," Maeve whispered to Avery.

"I love to read," Charlotte responded with enthusiasm while motioning for Avery and Maeve to be quiet. "I think that books are like best friends—they're always there when you need them."

"Well, little lady, there's a whole library back there of old books. But I don't go back there too much. Just not much of a reader."

"Wow!" Charlotte exclaimed. "Thanks, JT!" She charged out of the room with a backward wave to her friends. Old books were one of her all-time favorite things to explore.

The small room was covered in dust and grime. It was obvious that JT hadn't been there in a very long time. After whisking away giant curtains of cobwebs, Charlotte surveyed the shelves of books. There were hundreds of books—some in better shape than others, as JT had warned. Charlotte browsed the titles. There were a lot of famous early American classics, like Mark Twain's *Tom Sawyer* and Herman Melville's *Moby-Dick*, as well as some other old books that she'd never heard of.

Then she spied a rolltop desk in the corner. Charlotte loved rolltop desks with all their little cubbyholes and tiny drawers. Someday she wanted to have her own—a special desk where she'd do her best writing. She hesitated for a second—JT had said she could check out the library, but he hadn't given her permission to open the desk. Then again, he hadn't exactly said it was off limits either. A detective at heart, Charlotte couldn't resist. She started to pry the top open, but there was so much thick dust that she pulled her hands back. *Eeew.* The grime was so caked on that it seemed as if the desk hadn't been opened in years . . . decades, maybe. After rolling up her sleeves and with much rocking and prying, Charlotte was finally able to roll the top back.

As Charlotte explored the drawers and cubbyholes, an entire bank of drawers suddenly popped open. Charlotte's eyes widened. *A secret compartment—this is the kind of thing that only happens in the movies*, she thought.

Yuck! When she reached into the drawer, the first thing her hand brushed against was a dead spider. She gingerly brushed it away. No way was she going to let a little crunched up daddy-long-legs bother her . . . not after the scary spiders she had encountered in Africa.

Charlotte pulled out a stack of yellowed papers from the drawer and plopped into the wingback chair next to the window so she could get a better look. Immediately she realized this wasn't just another stack of old bills or hotel records. The papers were carefully hand-bound with string and a faded yellow ribbon. The package looked like a diary or a scrapbook of sorts, full of letters and mementos. Charlotte immediately became engrossed in the correspondence between a woman named Amaryllis, who had swooping, flowery handwriting, and a soldier who only signed his letters with one initial . . . she couldn't tell if it was *T* or *L.*

Charlotte's breath caught in her throat as she realized she was reading love letters between newlyweds. She felt a little funny reading such personal letters, but once she started she just *had* to know what happened next. The soldier, it seemed, was drafted to fight in the army toward the end of World War II.

Charlotte was spellbound by the beautiful handwriting and the obviously deep emotion that had brought pen to page. Amaryllis recorded the painful details of the mining disaster and how the town was totally devastated. No one had the strength to rebuild, particularly during the pinch of wartime. Sadly, only a week before the disaster, Amaryllis received a telegram from the government saying her dear husband was missing in action and presumed dead.

Charlotte brought a hand to her heart. It was as if she could feel just what Amaryllis had felt. She brushed away a few tears and swallowed hard before continuing to read. Amaryllis wrote that she had been so disturbed to receive the telegram that she burned the letter, refusing to believe it. She swore that she would have known in her heart if her true love had died.

Charlotte let the brittle pages fall to her lap and stared out the window. *Will I ever love someone that much?* she wondered. So much that even if he were half a world away, I would know whether or not he was alive?

Charlotte read on, eager to learn if Amaryllis's instincts had been correct. She wished with all her heart that Amaryllis would be reunited with her beloved.

But Charlotte soon read that Amaryllis had other

worries. State officials feared for the safety of Dry Gulch and its citizens and ordered a complete evacuation. Amaryllis wanted desperately to wait at home for her soldier husband's return, but she was expecting a child and had to think of the baby's safety. So she packed up and sought shelter with her parents in Kansas.

"There you are."

Charlotte almost jumped out of her seat, she was so startled. Maeve poked her head in the library door. "I've been looking all over for you. You've been gone for the longest time." Twisting a curl between her fingers, Maeve began to stammer. "Char, I was kind of wondering if you'd noticed anything . . . well, anything *strange* about your dad . . ." Maeve's voice trailed off when she noticed Charlotte's tear-stained face.

Charlotte had tried to wipe the tears away, but it was obvious that she'd been crying.

"Oh, Charlotte, what's wrong?" Maeve asked, putting her arm comfortingly around Charlotte. Expecting her friend to break down and sob, Maeve furrowed her brows in confusion when Charlotte burst into laughter instead.

"I'm just being sentimental," Charlotte confided. "Look at this."

She handed Maeve the delicate diary.

"A diary . . . a secret diary?" Maeve's eyes lit up and she sunk into the chair, eagerly flipping through the pages.

"What's going on?" Avery asked as she burst into the dusty old library.

"Avery, you HAVE to read this," Maeve insisted.

"Read what?" she asked.

"Charlotte found this old diary with love letters and everything," Maeve said, holding up the stack of papers. She stopped suddenly and stared down at the diary. "You know what this means?!" Maeve exclaimed.

Avery and Charlotte just looked at Maeve quizzically and shook their heads.

"We have just discovered our very own tragic-to-magic love story," Maeve said very seriously. She began pacing the room like a great tragic actress as she filled in the missing pieces of the story with her own ideas.

"This poor, war-weary soldier probably came back from the war and couldn't find his precious wife. I bet Amaryllis—what a lovely musical name that is!—AMA-RYLLLISSSSS!" Maeve sang out in a fake opera voice.

Avery plugged her ears with her fingers. "I could do without the concert," she moaned while Charlotte giggled at her dramatic friend. Nobody could tell a story like Maeve.

Maeve went on without missing a beat. "Sweet, lovely Amaryllis had their darling baby and he didn't even know anything about it and then years and years later, they FOUND each other again and rediscovered the magic of their young love and lived happily ever after. MAGIC!"

"WHOA!" Avery shouted and stopped Maeve mid-sentence. "Hey, Cinderella! Aren't you getting a little carried away with this fairy tale? How do you know that this soldier guy actually made it back from the war? It says right there that he was MIA—missing in action!"

"Hello! Things get really messed up in war." Maeve looked at her friends. "Besides, that's the way all great love stories go. The unimaginable happens, and people who are MEANT to be together . . . well, they just ARE!"

"All right, all right," Charlotte held up her hand. "Love conquers all." Charlotte flipped through the diary again. "What do you guys think this guy's initial is? I can't tell . . . *T? L?*"

Avery studied it closely. "Looks like a *J* to me. My grandfather on my dad's side is named John, and his handwriting kind of looked like this. Yeah, that's what his *J*s looked like. *J* is a pretty common first letter for a man's name. I mean, *J* could stand for John, Jim, Josh, or Joe."

"It could stand for Jeremiah or Jonah or Jake," Charlotte pointed out.

"Justin, Jacque, Jerry, Jay, Jeffrey, Jordan, Jesse, Joel, Juan, or Jebediah," Avery rattled off the names in quick succession as she leaped around the room.

Maeve and Charlotte laughed so hard at Avery's antics that there were tears in their eyes.

"Maeve," Charlotte said when they calmed down. "I think the point is that it's a great story, but I'm not convinced that 'J' lived happily ever after. Let's keep looking. Maybe we can find out more about J and Amaryllis. There're a lot of old papers in this desk."

The three searched through all the drawers until at last Charlotte pulled out a letter. "Wait, here's something! Oh, look! It's from the army. It's addressed to someone named Sergeant Jasper Tucker and it's a notification that his wife, Amaryllis Lockhart Tucker, and her parents, Ebenezer Lockhart and Priscilla Evans Lockhart, died in a car accident in January 1945."

"I was right!" said Avery. "The initial was *J* . . . *J* for Jasper. And Jehoshaphat," she giggled.

"Jasper Tucker," Charlotte said slowly. "Jasper Tucker. JT. JT. JT!" she repeated, the excitement growing in her voice as the pieces fell into place.

"JT?!" Maeve and Avery exclaimed.

"You mean, you think Jasper Tucker is our JT?" Maeve asked in wonder.

"Why not?" Charlotte asked. "It makes sense, right?! We know he grew up here and came back after the war. He must have tried to track his wife down, but when he got this letter saying she had died—"

"He had nothing left to live for!" Maeve interrupted dramatically, clasping her hands to her heart. "And he's been alone in this ghost town ever since, pining away for his lost love . . . and making fabulous chili."

"Should we tell JT about the diary?" Avery asked as she tried to stifle a giggle. *Maeve is just too funny sometimes*, she thought.

Charlotte looked reluctant. "I'm not sure. I mean, I don't know how I would feel about someone digging into MY past. Maybe he already knows everything. He might have read the diary before and tucked it away because it was all too painful to think about."

"But he's got to have relatives somewhere. He can't be totally alone in the world, right?" Maeve asked.

"I think we should talk to my dad about the whole thing before we say anything to JT," Charlotte said.

"Before we do anything else, I want to stop by the fireplace and thaw out. I'm freezing!" Maeve declared.

"Me too. My fingers are completely numb," Charlotte agreed, as she stood up and stretched.

"Really?" Avery asked. "I'm not cold at all. I think I'm going to jump around in the snowbanks for a while. Have you seen how huge some of them are?"

Avery ran out the front door and took a flying leap into a giant pile of snow. She was climbing out when a shadow fell across the snow bank. Avery looked up, and all she could see was a familiar cowboy hat.

"JT?" she said.

"You want to see about those howling noises?" he asked in his low, growling voice.

Avery couldn't stand up and scramble out of the snowdrift fast enough.

17

Four-Legged Secret

*I*T MIGHT BE OLD, thought Avery, *but he sure is fast.*
"Almost there," JT shouted, looking back at Avery, who
was trotting double-time to keep up with his long-
legged strides.

The snow was waist deep in places, and even with the
snowshoes she borrowed from JT, Avery was breathless
from trudging over the drifts. The two hikers passed piles
of rubble from the buildings that had collapsed during the
mine explosion more than sixty years earlier. Avery felt
sad for all the miners and their families. Finally, trudging
around the last pile of rocks, she spotted the entrance to
the mine. It was all boarded up, but there was something
yowling mournfully from the inside.

The hairs on the back of Avery's neck rose while a spark
of excitement ran through her veins. She was a little scared,
but mostly she was curious. What was behind that door?

"Ain't nothing to be 'fraid of," JT told her, reaching
into a nook and pulling out a key on a long chain.

The yips and barks reached a fevered pitch as JT worked the padlock. As soon as it was unlocked, he roughly shouldered the door open and disappeared inside.

Timidly, Avery crept closer to the door. Once inside, she saw there was a kennel with four cages. In each cage were some puppies . . . strange-looking puppies with intelligent and watchful eyes.

"What kind of dogs are those?" Avery asked. "They look kind of like Siberian huskies. Are they . . . ?"

"They ain't dogs. Those be wolf pups," JT said matter-of-factly.

Avery's eyes widened and her heart began thumping rapidly. "Where did the wolves come from?" she asked in a high-pitched voice. She had never seen a wolf up close before. She couldn't wait to tell her brothers and friends about this.

JT didn't answer. The wolf pups jumped at the wire walls of their cages, begging to be set free.

"Can I touch them?" Avery reached her hand toward the nearest cage.

JT grabbed her wrist and pulled it back roughly.

"I wouldn't be doin' that," he warned. "They is probably healthy enough . . . likely not to have rabies and all . . . but best to be careful. I got a vet friend who is sworn to secrecy 'bout this . . . like yourself now. She's coming out next week to take a look at them."

"Are you going to keep them?" Avery asked, kneeling down and staring at the pups, which were jumping and rolling over each other. She'd give anything to hold one of those soft bundles of fur.

"Wolves don't belong to no one. They are wild things. They belong in the wild." JT spoke gruffly.

"But JT, why aren't they in the wild, then? Where did they come from?"

"I found them abandoned a couple weeks back. I reckon their mother's dead. Killed, most likely," JT surmised.

The pups whined and yipped as if to agree with what he'd said.

"There's no one else who'd help these wild critters. I keep them here and tend to them. I couldn't leave them to die. Them's too young to make it on their own."

"But why does it have to be a secret?" Avery wondered.

"Wolves aren't welcome in these parts. If the ranchers found out there was wolves about, there'd be trouble. *Don't* want no trouble," said JT, shaking his head. "No trouble at all."

"But these little guys couldn't hurt . . ."

JT cut her off. "You don't understand. Folks in these parts don't care for wolves, pups or grown. Livestock is what people care about. Ranchers probably killed these pups' mother 'cause they figured she might go after one of their cattle."

Avery gulped. "I thought wolves were an endangered species in Montana."

"Some places they are. But them ranchers don't care none. They think the wolves are a threat to their livestock and to their family's livelihood."

Avery nodded. She was a total maniac for animals,

so it was hard for her to understand how someone could think of the furry creatures as a threat.

"My vet friend, she lives over by the border and helps the park service with wolf relocation. But she tells me funding's low. Them little guys just got to hang on a little while longer till she can get them out of here."

"Did you name them?" Avery asked.

"Sure thing. The boy there, he's Jake, and the others are Candice and Marylyn. And that small gray one is my favorite—she's Amaryllis."

Avery's mouth dropped open. Had he said *Amaryllis*? Like the lady from the diary Charlotte found? She was just about to ask JT about the unusual name when the door burst open.

Avery's heart leaped to her throat. She was terrified that the ranchers had found out about the wolf pups in hiding, but was quickly relieved to see it was just Mr. Ramsey.

Mr. Ramsey was breathing hard, like he'd been running. His cheeks were bright red and his breath was coming out of his mouth in quick puffs of steam.

"WHAT is going on here?!" Mr. Ramsey demanded. His eyebrows were knit together in a scowl. Avery had never seen Mr. Ramsey this angry before. He usually seemed so laid back, and even if he was annoyed, he never shouted or anything. Something had made Mr. Ramsey flip out big time.

JT must have been shocked, too, because he just stood there staring at Mr. Ramsey.

"I asked you a question, JT!" Mr. Ramsey spat out. "You don't take a twelve-year-old girl on a hike without asking permission. That is completely unacceptable!"

"He didn't mean to, Mr. Ramsey. It's not JT's fault. He was just showing me these wolf pups. He knows I love animals, and I was asking about the howling noises. I should have told you I was going on a hike with JT. I'm sorry. It's MY fault." Avery felt horrible. Now that she stopped to think, it was a pretty bad idea to go off alone with some person she barely knew, even if he didn't mean any harm.

"Avery, you SHOULD have known better. But JT is an adult, and he DEFINITELY should have known better."

JT looked utterly desolate. "I'm sorry. I been away from folks so long that sometimes I forget how to act. I'm right sorry. I made a big mistake."

Seeing that Avery was fine and how ashamed JT was, Mr. Ramsey calmed down a bit, and Avery filled him in on the plight of the wolf pups.

"Is it common for the ranchers to kill wolves?" Mr. Ramsey asked.

JT shook his head. "Don't know about that. I just try to look after any pups whenever I find 'em out here. But I can only do so much, you see."

"Mr. Ramsey, since you're a writer, maybe you can do something. Could you write an article about the wolves so people will know about their problems?" Avery suggested.

Mr. Ramsey smiled and patted the hood of Avery's snow parka. "Always thinking, Avery. We'll see what we can do. Let's go, now. Time to get back to the others."

JT sat down on a chair he had carved out of a tree

stump. "You go on ahead. I'll be back in a bit. I got to check in with the pups first."

The Flickering Candle

"Real live wolf pups?" Maeve asked incredulously.

Avery nodded. "And I have even *bigger* news."

"What?" Charlotte asked.

"One of the pups is named Amaryllis," Avery announced, crossing her arms in front of her.

"Amaryllis. Just like in the diary," Charlotte mused. "Well, if that's not proof that JT is our mystery man, I don't know what is!"

"What are you kids talking about?" Mr. Ramsey asked, looking suspiciously at the girls.

"Come on, Dad. I'll show you," Charlotte insisted, pulling her father to his feet and leading him to the library. She told him to sit in the wingback chair next to the window and brought over the hand-bound diary and stack of letters. The three girls watched him, hoping for a glimpse of understanding, as he scanned the material.

Mr. Ramsey looked up after he had perused much of the diary. "Well, I think we can be fairly certain that this Jasper Tucker is our JT. Seems like it's more than a coincidence that everything is fitting together."

"It's just so sad that he's living here all alone, Dad. Do you think he has any family that could take care of him? He's getting pretty old."

Mr. Ramsey nodded and stared out the window at the fading daylight. "Yes. Yes, I think we can help JT."

They heard JT come through the front door, and everyone slipped back into the parlor.

"I was wondering if the girls wanted to help me cook up some grub for the wolves," JT said. "I mean, if that'd be fine with you, Mr. Ramsey."

Mr. Ramsey nodded. "It's fine. But I'll come with you. I'm responsible for the girls, so I need to keep an eye on them. And actually, I'm kind of curious to learn more about these wolves myself."

The girls and Mr. Ramsey layered on their winter gear and followed JT through the kitchen. They took beef from the meat locker outside and gathered canned goods from the pantry. They packed all the food into old hiking backpacks, strapped on snowshoes, and began the steep, snowy climb.

"So, JT," Charlotte said as she trudged through the deep snow. "It's the pups that have been howling in the night, right? They're the ones that have been keeping us awake?"

"Nope," was JT's only response.

"No?" Avery paused, looking puzzled as she shifted her backpack.

"Not entirely. Them pups is too little to make so much noise. They just whine and yip most of the time."

"Then what's all the howling we've been hearing?"

"I reckon it's adult wolves, over yonder in the hills."

"See, I told you," Avery reminded Charlotte and Maeve.

"I saw some tracks behind the old outhouse this morning," JT said. "Looked like wolf tracks to me."

"Behind the outhouse? But that's practically at the backdoor!" Maeve cried.

"Yup," JT agreed.

"So you're saying there are all kinds of wild animals ready to attack us at any moment?" Maeve asked.

"They curious, is all," JT said. "Snow kills the smell of humans and makes them a little bolder. Braver."

Maeve glanced over her right shoulder and then her left. "I don't like this one bit," she said. "But you're a real mountain man, right, JT?"

JT looked at Maeve as if she was more than a bit crazy.

"I mean you can scare off wolves and grizzly bears. They're afraid of you, right?" Maeve asked.

"Why, that's right!" JT said. "I've fought off grizzlies with my bare hands," he added.

"Really?" Maeve could hardly believe it.

"Why, sure. One grizzly bear even took a chunk out of my shoulder once," he said, winking at Charlotte and Avery.

"It did? Then what happened?" Maeve was in total awe at JT's tall tales.

"He spit it right back out. I'm too tough and bitter to be good. Them grizzlies pretty much leave me alone now." JT winked again at Avery and Charlotte, and they struggled to fight back the giggles. Mr. Ramsey couldn't help chuckling, but Maeve didn't seem to notice.

"But don't you worry about a thing," JT reassured Maeve. "You just stick close to me—the mountain man, as you say. Those beasts don't want to get too close to an ornery ole cuss like me."

From that moment on Maeve stayed as close as she could to JT. It was like she was attached to his left arm.

As they walked into the mine entrance, the girls dropped everything and ran to the cages.

"Hold up!" Mr. Ramsey said firmly. "Don't get too close. Those wolf pups look cute, but they're wild animals, girls. Step back."

After cooing and fussing over the very cute wolf pups—at a safe distance—the girls helped JT stack the food at the entrance to the abandoned mine.

"I reckon we brought enough food to last a month or so," JT said as he surveyed the supply.

"The kids back at school are NOT going to believe that we saw wild wolf pups. And helped save their lives!" Charlotte exclaimed.

"JT, maybe if you and your vet friend could bring wolf pups into classrooms to teach kids about them, people would start to care more and the ranchers wouldn't get away with killing them," Avery suggested.

JT chuckled at the thought of taking one of the rambunctious pups to a school. "That's an idea, sure it is. But most folks wouldn't let some old mountain man into their school with a wild wolf pup. I'd have to belong to some wildlife society, I reckon."

"Society schmiety," Maeve chanted. "You practically ARE wildlife, JT!" Maeve immediately clapped her hands over her mouth. *Maybe I shouldn't have said that . . .*

But JT just chuckled. He reached into the kennel, grabbed one of the pups by the scruff of his neck, and supported him under the hind legs so he could change the wolf's bandage.

Maeve kept her distance. She was genuinely afraid of the wolf pups. Even though they were supercute and fluffy, there was an aura of wildness about them. Charlotte and Avery, on the other hand, jumped right in to help. Avery wordlessly handed bandages to JT, and Charlotte was ready with the antibiotic ointment. Not wanting to be left out, Maeve helped Mr. Ramsey arrange the canned food in piles.

JT returned the wolf pup to the cage. "Thank ya kindly for helping me out. It would have taken me a long time to bring all this food up by m'self."

JT motioned for the others to head out the mineshaft door ahead of him and paused for a moment to stare at the pups before he firmly shut the door and secured it. The group started the long trek down the hill. JT's steps were slow and his breathing labored.

"Are you feeling all right, JT?" Mr. Ramsey asked. "Maybe we should rest for a few minutes."

"No, best to keep moving," JT shook his head.

When they finally reached town, JT gave them a salute and disappeared through the servant's entrance of the Hotel de Paris. The girls stood motionless in the snow, watching him lumber off.

"I think maybe living in this ghost town by himself is too much for an eighty-year-old," Charlotte said.

"It does seem that living out here has taken a toll on him," Mr. Ramsey agreed. "All right, girls, I'm going to walk to the edge of town and see if there's any sign of a rescue team. I should be back in an hour or so. Stay at the hotel or close by. And don't go off alone. Buddy system is in full effect."

Avery, Charlotte, and Maeve headed back into the sitting room of the hotel. They took off their coats but left on sweatshirts and scarves to keep away the chill. Charlotte disappeared into the library, while Maeve and Avery plopped down on the couch and just looked at each other.

"There HAS to be something else to do in this old place. Didn't people have ANY fun before the twenty-first century?" Avery complained.

Maeve giggled. "Avery, WE lived in the twentieth century for a while."

"Whatever. You know what I mean." Avery started opening cupboards and drawers, searching for something—anything—to cure their boredom.

"Jackpot!" Avery cried, holding up a deck of cards that she'd pulled from the very back of a drawer.

"Let's play Spit!" Maeve suggested. The two of them began to play one of their favorite Tower card games. Avery was supercompetitive, but Maeve was enthusiastic and determined to win as well. The game got faster and faster as they slapped cards down and arranged the piles.

"I'm getting hungry for dinner," Avery announced finally, throwing her cards down. "Hey, I wonder what Lissie's doing? I thought she'd be making dinner by now or something. Let's go over to the store. I want to get some more of that boxed milk."

"Char!" Maeve called. "We're going to the store . . . come on!"

As soon as they were out the door, Maeve linked arms with her two friends.

"What are you doing, Maeve?" Avery asked.

"Buddy system. Just like Mr. Ramsey said," Maeve grinned. "I don't want to lose my buddies."

As they moved off in the direction of the General Store, lights began to flicker in one of the houses at the edge of Main Street.

"Look, look!" Avery cried.

"Yeah, that's a cool old place," Maeve said. "That cottage is falling apart, but you can tell it used to be beautiful. Lissie said it was a wrecked version of her dream house."

"No, I meant the *lights*!" Avery pointed.

Maeve stopped dead in her tracks and stared at the cottage windows.

"Maybe there really are ghosts in Dry Gulch," Charlotte shivered.

"Let's go," Avery insisted, pulling them forward.

As soon as they crossed the street, all three girls stared up at the little cottage again. Sure enough, a candle flickered in the window.

"Do you think JT has other friends around here he hasn't told us about?" Maeve whispered.

"I'm kind of worried that they're not friends. What if some crazy escaped convict is hiding out in this town, too?" Charlotte asked.

Cautiously, the girls crept to the front door. As they got closer, they heard laughter coming from inside. Quietly, they stole into the front room. It was dark, but through the crack of a barely open door, a wedge of flickering light spilled from the next room.

Charlotte tiptoed across the floor, half terrified and half

excited to discover what was to come. Halfway across the room, she stepped on a loose floorboard, which sounded a long *creeeaaak*. Instinctively, Charlotte froze in her tracks, but it was too late. Whoever was in the candlelit room had stopped talking.

"Who's there?" a woman called out.

The door flew open and a shadow filled the doorway.

All three girls gasped and Charlotte jumped back, but when her eyes adjusted to the light, Charlotte saw that it wasn't the shadow of a strange man—it was her father.

Charlotte peered over her father's shoulder and there, sitting at a tiny table set for two, was Lissie.

CHAPTER

18

Discovering Lissie

*A*very and Maeve giggled with relief, but Charlotte's cheeks burned bright red. Lissie looked dazzling in the candlelight. Could it be she was glowing with true love?

"We were just having a little dinner. I met Lissie on my way out of town and she said she was cooking up a surprise," Mr. Ramsey explained.

"A romantic, candlelit dinner surprise," Charlotte heard Maeve whisper to Avery.

"Come in. Come in!" Mr. Ramsey motioned for the girls to join them.

"Yes, girls. Come join us! I was going to come find you in a few minutes. I made beef stroganoff for all of us. Well, makeshift beef stroganoff. Without the noodles." Lissie pointed to the pot in front of her.

"We don't want to *interrupt*," Maeve stressed. "I mean, it looks like this is a table for two," she said, shooting Avery a knowing look.

Charlotte couldn't speak. She couldn't even move. The romantic scene before her eyes left her utterly speechless.

"I have something to tell you girls," Mr. Ramsey said, sitting at the table and grabbing Lissie's hand.

He was holding her hand. Charlotte couldn't believe her eyes.

"Girls, I want you to meet someone very special," Mr. Ramsey said.

The words jolted Charlotte from her frozen spot on the floor. Without a second thought, she leaped into the candlelit room. "No, Dad! You've known her less than a week!"

Lissie and Mr. Ramsey stared at Charlotte and then looked at each other in a stunned moment of silence. Then they both burst into laughter.

"Oh, Charlotte. What did you think I was going to say?" Mr. Ramsey asked. "That Lissie and I were going to get married or something?" He couldn't help but chuckle again. When he saw that Charlotte was truly upset, though, he put his arm around her.

Charlotte was a jumble of emotions. All at once she was embarrassed, relieved, and mostly hurt. After all, her father and this woman they barely knew were laughing at her.

"It's really not funny," Charlotte insisted.

"I'm sorry, Charlotte. It was just the look on your face that made us laugh." Mr. Ramsey looked genuinely sorry as he explained this, and Lissie was actually starting to look kind of embarrassed.

Good, Charlotte thought. You should be embarrassed

that you are trying to woo my father with beef stroganoff and flickering candles!

Mr. Ramsey collected himself and took a deep breath. "Lissie and I are just friends. We have a lot of the same interests and enjoy each other's company," he said, smiling at Lissie. "Contrary to popular opinion, men and women are quite capable of being friends." He paused as he looked pointedly at Maeve and Avery. "Even when there are candles involved. How else would we see what we were eating?"

Maeve and Avery shrugged and shook their heads, and Charlotte just waited for her dad to continue.

"Lissie and I were just talking about her family and stories about growing up. That's all," Mr. Ramsey explained honestly.

Charlotte's sigh of relief was so big that everyone burst out laughing again, and even Charlotte joined in this time. *I guess it WAS kind of funny*, she thought.

"Why don't you all sit down?" Lissie said, pulling a few more chairs up to the table. "Where's JT? He must be hungry by now, too."

Charlotte opened her mouth to answer, but her father interrupted her.

"What I was starting to say before is that I have a very interesting announcement," he began.

The girls leaned forward expectantly.

Charlotte wondered if her dad had gotten a call on his cell phone saying that a rescue team was on its way.

Maeve wondered if Mr. Ramsey was going to tell them that because they'd become close friends, Lissie was going to change her plans and move to Boston.

Avery wondered if Lissie and Mr. Ramsey had found a frozen pizza somewhere and were baking it in the oven.

"Girls, I'd like you to meet Amaryllis," Mr. Ramsey announced grandly.

The girls looked around, visibly confused.

"What?" Charlotte shrugged.

"Who?" Maeve wondered.

"Where?!" Avery demanded.

Lissie pointed to herself. "I'm Amaryllis. Lissie for short. Amaryllis is my grandmother's name."

Someone gasped, and Charlotte looked around the room to see where it came from. She was surprised to see JT standing in the doorway of the small, candlelit room. "Your grandmother's name was Amaryllis?" JT asked. "That's . . . that's a very unusual name," he stuttered.

Lissie nodded. "My grandmother moved away from Montana at the end of World War II. Her husband was a soldier fighting in the war, but then was listed as missing in action and presumed dead. My grandmother was pregnant with my mother at the time, and she went to live with her parents so she wouldn't be alone. But her parents died a couple of months later in a car accident."

JT's face went ghostly white. He looked as if he might fall down and grabbed the doorframe for support. Instinctively, Charlotte and Maeve both rushed to his side, and the two girls helped him to a chair.

"What was your grandmother's name? Her full name," JT managed to ask.

"Amaryllis Lockhart Tucker," Lissie told him.

JT slowly shook his head. "It can't be. But . . . I thought . . . I got a letter from the Army . . ."

"It's true!" Charlotte cried out. "You see, I found this diary . . ." Charlotte took the diary from her inside coat pocket and laid it on the table in front of JT.

His fingers fumbled with the pages. "My eyesight ain't what it used to be," he mumbled. "Can't see much print anymore."

"The diary says that some guy named J's wife—Amaryllis—was pregnant when the mine disaster struck," Avery burst in. "She wanted to wait around in case J came back from the war, but she had to leave with her family to take care of her baby."

JT stared first at Avery and then at Charlotte. "How in the world," JT started, but he was too flustered to finish.

"I found the diary and the letters in the library," Charlotte explained. "I know I shouldn't have gone through the desk, but I just couldn't help myself. It was like discovering a museum right in the Hotel de Paris. And I didn't want to tell you what I found—I thought it might stir up painful memories. And it wasn't until right now that we found out that . . . that Lissie must be your granddaughter."

"You're not alone, Jasper," Maeve smiled at him. "You have a family."

No one said anything, and the only sound was the soft flicker of the candle flame.

From the look on her face, Charlotte could tell that Lissie was as shocked as JT. Finally, Lissie was able to speak. "I didn't know what town my grandmother came from or anything about the mining disaster, except what I've read on my own. Gram always talks about life in Montana, but never the bad things that happened to her. From what I know of the family history, my grandmother remarried when my mother was twelve."

Charlotte watched JT's face. It was obvious that JT had thought his wife, Amaryllis Tucker, had been dead for years.

"My grandmother was widowed a few years ago," Lissie added.

"A few years ago?" JT asked, finding it difficult to keep up with the story that was unfolding. "But I got a letter sayin' she an' her parents were . . . that there was a car accident . . ."

"We saw that letter, too," Charlotte added, putting it all together. "But now we know it must have been a terrible mistake! Just like the letter that she got saying you were missing in action!"

JT shook his head slowly, trying to sort everything out. "So . . . if she were widowed a few years ago . . . you mean she was still alive a few years ago?"

"She's still alive now," Lissie said softly. She reached over and patted JT's arm.

"And she's going to be thrilled when I call to tell her that I've found you."

JT's mouth dropped open, but no sound came out. Happy tears welled in his eyes.

"Grandma hoped for so long that you would come back," Lissie assured him. "She refused to believe that you were gone. She will be so overjoyed to learn that her heart was telling her the truth."

JT shakily raised a hand to his eye and wiped a tear away with the tip of his finger. "To think, I was here the whole time . . ." an emotional JT whispered.

Mr. Ramsey rose from his chair and ushered the girls from the room to leave the newfound grandfather and granddaughter alone.

The girls stepped out onto the wooden sidewalk outside the little cottage. Charlotte looked back through the growing darkness at the window of light. "Look! Look!" she pointed at the scene unfolding.

They saw Lissie and JT share a warm hug. JT patted Lissie on the cheek, and he looked really, truly happy.

"Wow!" Avery cried.

"It's all so heart-wrenching and tragic and romantic!" Maeve said as she feigned a swoon. "Totally out of a classic movie."

"He looks so genuinely happy," Charlotte said. "Without that permanent frown on his face, I almost don't recognize JT—oops, I mean *Jasper*."

"Jassssssssper." Avery giggled, rolling the strange, old-fashioned name around on her tongue. "Nah," she said decisively, shaking her head. "He'll always be plain old JT to me. That's what he told us to call him, right?"

"Shhh! Listen," Maeve demanded, cupping her ear. Since the town was silent, they could hear little bits of the conversation. They heard JT say that maybe it was time to stop living all alone in the ghost town. After all, he wasn't getting any younger.

Then they heard Lissie say that she'd be going back East from time to time to visit her family, and that JT should come with her to see what rural Vermont was like.

The girls could tell by the way JT nodded that he liked the idea, although they overheard him wonder who'd take care of the wolves.

Lissie promised that she and Mr. Ramsey would see what they could do to get the wolves a safe haven, if not here in Dry Gulch, then somewhere else.

"Really?" Avery asked Mr. Ramsey. "Can you really make that happen?"

Mr. Ramsey put a reassuring hand on Avery's shoulder.

"I promise, I'll do what I can, Avery."

19

Hope Drifts

The happy troop followed the pathway through the deep snow back to Main Street and the Hotel de Paris. It was late afternoon, and the darkness was growing.

Lissie joined them in the hotel a few minutes later. "My *grandfather*," she said, smiling at the new term, "is checking on the wolf pups back at the mine. He said he'd join us as soon as he's finished."

"Did you find any scrap paper in the library, Charlotte?" Mr. Ramsey asked.

Charlotte nodded. "Loads."

"I'm going to need some kindling to build up this fire."

Mr. Ramsey disappeared into the library, while Lissie served bowls of beef stroganoff to the girls. They were all famished after their hike and the long day, and no one spoke as they devoured the satisfying dinner.

Suddenly, they heard a sound—a faint whirring at first, but growing louder by the minute.

"What IS that?" Maeve asked.

Avery's face tensed up with concentration as she struggled to place the sound. "It's a helicopter!" she blurted out and jumped up as if she were a game show contestant who had just come up with the million dollar answer.

Mr. Ramsey raced out of the library and onto Main Street, the others at his heels.

Sure enough, a helicopter was circling the town. Against the night sky, it looked like an alien spaceship about to swoop down on Dry Gulch.

Everyone jumped up and down and waved their arms, trying to get the helicopter's attention.

"Save us, save us!" Maeve cried dramatically, flailing her arms in every direction.

"OVER HERE! OVER HERE!" Avery bounced up and down, throwing snowballs in the air.

The pilot signaled that he saw them and landed the helicopter just north of Main Street. He and an emergency medical person with a first aid kit and a stretcher climbed down and hurried to the little group to make sure everyone was okay.

"No injuries here, thank goodness," Mr. Ramsey assured them. "We're all just a little chilly but completely safe and sound."

"There's no way we can get you all on one chopper," the pilot told Mr. Ramsey. "Gather your things together. I'll get another guy in here."

The girls rushed into the hotel to pack their clothes. As Charlotte shoved her belongings into her backpack, she couldn't help feeling a bit sad at leaving the little ghost town. There was so much more to explore in Dry Gulch and in some ways it had started to feel like a second home.

Maeve and Avery, on the other hand, were already out the door.

"Come on, Charlotte," Avery called. "Let's get outta this place!"

Charlotte lingered for a moment, absorbing all the details of the room and imagining once more how it must have looked in the 1890s when it was a booming mining town. She could almost see the ghosts of Dry Gulch moving through this once busy hotel. She was definitely going to write about this place someday.

Avery appeared at the door. "Charlotte, hurry up! We're LEAVING!"

Charlotte picked up her backpack and slung it over her shoulder. There would always be ghosts here—ghosts of the people whose lives she never had a chance to learn about. But somehow Charlotte felt like she had freed the ghosts of Amaryllis and Jasper Tucker through uncovering the diaries and letters. Now they would be free to live in the present instead of pining away for the past.

Lissie and JT were standing on the sidewalk when Charlotte stepped over the threshold and closed the door to the Hotel de Paris.

"I . . . I don't know," JT was saying. "What about the wolves?" he asked Lissie. "It's hard enough leaving my home, but leaving the wolves to fend for themselves? No. No. It's too much."

Mr. Ramsey was quietly observing the conversation from across the street and motioned for JT to walk down the sidewalk with him. Mr. Ramsey talked in a low voice with JT as they walked. As much as she strained her ears, Charlotte could not hear what they were saying. But by the time they reached the end of the sidewalk, Jasper Tucker was ready to go. He had been convinced to step onto the helicopter and start another chapter of his life.

The girls strapped themselves into one helicopter with Mr. Ramsey, while Lissie and JT got into the second helicopter that had been called in.

Maeve was scared to death as the propellers whirred and the engines kicked up clouds of white snow.

"Owwwwww! Maeve! Let go of my arm! Your nails are digging into my skin!" Avery yelled, yanking her arm away from Maeve.

"Sorry," Maeve mumbled.

"Just shut your eyes and relax," Charlotte suggested.

Maeve squeezed her eyes shut and hummed "Oh, What a Beautiful Mornin'" to herself. The tune calmed her down, but having her eyes shut made her feel woozy.

"Airsick," Charlotte explained to her.

"I feel like I'm on a tilt-a-whirl," Maeve said, holding her head in her hands. "The whole world is spinning and tilting around and around."

"They call that vertigo. Just try to relax and breathe normally," Charlotte suggested, as she patted Maeve comfortingly on the back.

"Look! Hey, *look*!" Avery shouted. "There's the resort."

Big Sky Resort looked like a sparkling jewel set in the snow.

"Ohhhh! The lights on the snow are so romantic. It's beautiful!" Charlotte cried.

Maeve wanted to see, but she couldn't bear to open her eyes until she felt the helicopter land.

"Oh," Maeve gasped as the door opened and the icy cold air hit her face. It was a most welcoming and refreshing sensation. Maeve was relieved—and extremely thankful—that she hadn't thrown up. But her discomfort was immediately forgotten when she saw Katani and Isabel, and right behind them, Nik and Sam. Maeve rushed to her friends, hugging them first before gathering everyone into a group hug. It was wonderful to be reunited again.

Catching Up

"I can't believe how beautiful this is!" Maeve exclaimed, looking at the huge window in their suite. "High ceilings! Shiny wood floors! Stone fireplaces! And the bathroom! Did you see the bathroom, Charlotte?" Maeve asked, her voice echoing as she ducked her head into the enormous washroom.

"I saw it." Charlotte nodded, although she couldn't quite understand why Maeve was so excited by a bathroom.

"I swear the bathroom alone is the size of my dad's whole apartment!" Maeve marveled.

"A step above the Hotel de Paris?" Charlotte grinned.

"I feel like a princess." Maeve twirled around with arms in the air before flopping back on her bed. "And this princess is going to sleep well tonight!"

"Yeah! My back still hurts from camping out in the

hotel living room," Avery added. "Let's go hang out in the hot tub."

"I'm in!" Charlotte agreed.

"Get Nik and Sam to come over!" Maeve said, rushing to grab her bathing suit.

"I'll call their room!" Katani picked up the phone.

Mr. Ramsey turned on the hot tub, while the girls changed into their suits. They tiptoe-ran across the cold balcony, dropped their towels on the bench, and eased into the steamy, bubbling water.

"Ahhhh! This feels so *luxurious*!" Maeve squealed.

Moments later there was a knock at the door. Mr. Ramsey let the twins in, and they joined the group in the hot tub.

"All right, girls." Katani rested her arm on the side of the tub and turned to her friends. "Spill it. What in the world have you been doing since we last saw you?"

"Did you see any ghosts?" Isabel wanted to know.

Avery, Charlotte, and Maeve shared a look and giggled.

"One or two," Avery answered.

Maeve launched into a very lively, *slightly* exaggerated story about the days and nights they had spent in a real live ghost town.

Avery rolled her eyes when Maeve made it sound like she had single-handedly solved the mystery of Jasper Tucker and Amaryllis. "Maeve, Charlotte was the one that found all those diaries and figured out that Jasper Tucker was JT."

"I suppose," Maeve admitted. "But I did predict the

whole romance thing. You gotta give me that."

Charlotte was so happy to be hanging in the hot tub with the BSG that she didn't care if Maeve took ALL the credit for solving the mystery.

"We had a sleepover in Nik and Sam's room . . . with room service and everything!" Isabel announced.

"It was fab," Katani agreed.

"I hear you guys have sleepovers all the time in Charlotte's Tower," Nik said.

"It's not my Tower, it's our Tower," Charlotte corrected. "As far as I'm concerned, it belongs to all the BSG."

"I hope we'll get to go to a real BSG sleepover the next time we're in Boston," Sam said.

"You better!" Maeve grinned. "You guys have to meet Marty. And we'll bring you to Montoya's for the best hot chocolate you've ever had!"

"It feels like you girls have been here the whole time," Nik said to Maeve, Avery, and Charlotte.

"I know what you mean." Charlotte nodded. "It's like the past few days are a blur and all that matters is we're together again in this sweet suite!"

"Hey, look! It's snowing again!" Avery exclaimed. "I can't believe I'm in my bathing suit in the snow."

Everyone tilted their heads back and tried to catch the falling snowflakes on their tongues.

"I hope the snow doesn't delay that vet lady," Avery said, staring up into the dark sky.

"What vet lady?" Isabel asked.

"JT takes care of these abandoned wolf pups and—ahhh, cut it out!"

Maeve was waving her arms to stop Avery from talking, but she ended up splashing the whole group by mistake.

"Maeve!" Katani screeched.

"Sorry, it's just that we were supposed to keep it a secret—remember, Ave?" Maeve asked.

"Keep what a secret?" Isabel wondered.

"Next time, say it, don't spray it, Maeve. Just promise not to tell anyone else," Avery said to the others.

"We promise!" they chorused.

Avery, Maeve, and Charlotte took turns describing the sounds of the wolves howling in the night and helping JT feed the pups.

"The red wolf from Louisiana and Arkansas was down to a population of just eleven," Nik reported. "We learned about it in school. But they were able to get the population up and return them to the wild . . . mostly in the Appalachians."

"Nik and I love animals," Sam confided. "It makes me really mad to see them being treated badly."

Nik and Sam shared a long, thoughtful look and then nodded in unison.

"We'll have to check with our parents—" Nik started to say.

"—but maybe we can donate some of the proceeds from our concert—" Sam continued.

"—to a wildlife refuge that rescues animals—" Nik went on.

"—especially wolves," Sam finished.

"Hey, that's amazing!" Maeve exclaimed. "You guys

know what each other is thinking without even talking!"

"No, what's more amazing is that you guys are going to donate money to help the poor wolves. That's incredibly generous of you!" Avery gave each of the twins a high five.

"Look guys, I'm getting wrinkles," Maeve announced, holding up her water-logged fingers to the group. "I think it's time to get out. Dibs on first shower!"

Night Explorers

"Avery, where are you going?" Katani demanded as she watched Avery pull on her snow boots. "It's freezing outside and almost pitch black."

Avery threw on a neck warmer and grabbed her ski jacket. "The snow looks so fluffy and inviting. I need to check out the dogsledding ASAP. Did you see the write-up about it in the info packet?" she asked.

"Yeah," Isabel replied. "I thought that'd be your kind of thing."

"Come on, guys. It's time to go exploring," Avery said with a mischievous grin.

"But . . ." Katani protested, looking longingly at the comfy leather couch.

"Come on! How many times do you get the chance to see a real dogsled team?" Avery asked, throwing Katani's jacket on top of her head.

"I can't believe I'm doing this," Maeve groaned as she started pulling on warm clothes. "I didn't think I'd want to even look at snow for a very long time."

"We only have two days left, so we gotta make the

most of it. I want to see those dogs NOW!"

"I'm in," Charlotte chimed, wrapping a scarf around her neck. "Let me just leave a note for Dad."

"What's taking you guys so long?" Avery bounced up and down impatiently. "All right, I'm out. Meet you guys in front of the kennel."

Avery stopped short when she saw a majestic group of dogs hitched up at the kennel gate. "Wow! These guys are amazing," she exclaimed.

The mush master smiled. "Let me introduce you," she said. "Over here we have the Siberian huskies: Juno, Sasha, Silver, Nikki, Angel, and Kyra. And on this side we have the Alaskan malamutes: Storm, Tasha, Misha, Tundra, Max, and Cody. And I'm Marissa."

"Wow," was all Avery could croak out as she admired the gorgeous dogs. She still considered Marty to be the best dog in the world, but these dogs were very impressive.

"Are you thinking of going on a dogsled trek?" Marissa asked.

Avery nodded enthusiastically. "Yeah. We're here for a couple more days and that's the only thing I HAVE to do."

"With six dogs pulling, they can hit twenty miles per hour," Marissa told her.

"Really? That's pretty fast!"

"Yeah, you have to hang on around the corners," Marissa told them.

By then, the rest of the girls had caught up and Avery set about introducing her friends to the dogs.

". . . And that one's Cody," Avery rattled off.

"We'll have to bring the camera tomorrow and take lots of pictures for Marty," Charlotte suggested. "Hey, Ave . . . where are you going?"

"Back to the suite! The sooner we get to bed, the sooner we can get up and hang out with those pups!" she called back, tearing off her hat and gloves as she sprinted toward the main building.

CHAPTER

20

Front Row Center

"Pinch me," Katani said to Isabel as they walked into the greenroom behind Big Sky's Missouri Ballroom. "I can't believe our luck!"

"I know. Who else do we know that's been invited *backstage* at a big concert?" Isabel asked. "We're totally VIP."

The twins had asked Katani and Isabel to meet them backstage and help them get ready for their performance. Maeve had pouted for fifteen whole minutes when she found out, but the excitement of the concert got the better of her and now she was happily waiting for the show to start from her front row seat.

Nik and Sam paused their vocal warm-up when they noticed Katani and Isabel standing at the door. "Hey, girls! Perfect timing . . . did we tie these scarves right?" Nik pointed to the Kgirl accessory that she'd looped through her jeans.

"You girls look amazing," Katani said. "You don't even need our help, but we're here for you . . . ICFE."

"ICFE?" Isabel looked puzzled.

"In case of fashion emergency," Katani explained.

"Izzy, we were hoping you would come up onstage and help us sing 'Every Little Step' just like you did at rehearsal," Sam urged sweetly.

Isabel's cheeks immediately turned crimson. "Uh, thanks for the offer, but I don't think I'm cut out for the stage. Rehearsal is one thing, but . . . did you see all those people out there?!"

"Okay, okay! We won't make you," Nik said with a grin. "But just remember, we want you up there!"

"Break a leg." Katani linked her arm through Nik's, who linked her arm through Isabel's, who linked her arm through Sam's.

"Thanks for everything!" the twins cried.

Isabel looked at her watch. "We'd better get to our seats before the show starts. See you after!"

"Can you believe these seats?" Maeve asked Isabel and Katani as they sat down.

"That's about the two hundredth time Maeve has said that." Charlotte grinned.

At that moment the lights went down and everyone cheered as Nik and Sam walked onstage. The BSG barely sat down during the entire concert. Mostly they were up on their feet—dancing, singing along, and clapping like crazy.

"We'd like to dedicate this song to our new friends Katani, Isabel, Maeve, Avery, and Charlotte. We love you guys!" Nik and Sam pointed to the front row.

"They say I'm a wild child . . ." the song began.

The BSG cheered for their favorite song.

"'Old Enough' rocks!" Avery shouted.

When the twins took their final bows and exited the stage, the BSG finally flopped back in their seats.

"I'm exhausted!" Maeve exclaimed. "But it was TOTALLY worth it."

Just then an usher handed Mr. Ramsey a note. "Too bad you're so tired." Mr. Ramsey folded the note and put it in his pocket. "Because we've been invited to a VIP after-party. But if you don't think you're up for it . . ."

"Me, tired?!" Maeve asked as she popped to her feet. "I'm wide awake! Take me to the party!"

Mr. Ramsey led the way down the main corridor of Big Sky Resort and into a glitzy room decked out in fancy tablecloths, yellow roses, and twinkling lights.

"Look! There are so many famous people here!" Maeve cried.

"Over there! Is that . . . ? I love her!" Isabel pointed.

"This is the best day of my life," Maeve declared. "I can't believe all the celebrities I've seen now!"

Nik and Sam's mom rushed over to welcome the girls. "I'm glad you could make it. Katani, the girls' outfits are inspired! You do great work. I bet you'll be a top designer."

"Thank you. That's my goal." Katani nodded.

"Is *that* Megan Elizabeth and Liza May from the Rocking Cowgirls?" Maeve knew it was rude, but she couldn't help pointing.

"Yes. Nik and Sam were so excited they showed up! Some of the country stars were touring in the area and they stopped to check out the concert," Nik and Sam's mom told them. "Now, please don't be shy . . . go have something to eat."

"Thanks!" Avery called. She was already halfway to the buffet.

Love Conquers All

It had been a long day, and Charlotte's mind was still whirling even when she was getting ready for bed. She remembered that the twins had asked her to give them information about JT and the wolf pups. Nik, Sam, and the crew were leaving early the next day to continue their tour. Charlotte wasn't sure she would see them in the morning, so she quickly jotted down the information and slipped out the door to tiptoe to the twins' suite. Charlotte looked at her watch . . . 10:21 p.m. She thought it might be too late to knock, so she just slid the note under their door.

"Charlotte! What are you doing?" The booming voice in the empty hallway startled her.

"Dad! You scared me. I was just leaving the twins a note about the wolf pups," she explained. "You're not mad that I snuck out for a few minutes, are you?"

"No. I heard the door open, and I just wanted to make sure you were all right," he said.

"I'm fine."

"Look, honey, I wanted to apologize for what happened yesterday," Mr. Ramsey began.

Charlotte wanted to tell him that apologizing wasn't necessary; she was fine. But the truth was, having her father and Lissie laugh at her worries had hurt—even if it was silly. The words gathered in her throat, but all she could do was swallow hard.

Charlotte's dad enfolded her into a warm, comforting hug that immediately calmed her down.

"You shouldn't have to apologize," Charlotte told her dad, surprised at how casual she sounded. "I know you probably want a girlfriend someday. That's totally normal."

Mr. Ramsey held Charlotte at arm's length and studied her face. Slowly, a bright smile spread across his face.

"Maybe someday," he said as he ruffled her hair.

The two turned and slowly walked back toward the suite where the rest of the girls were waiting.

"Dad, what's going to happen to the wolf pups?" Charlotte asked.

"Well, as you know," Mr. Ramsey started slowly, "Lissie is going to be working here at Big Sky Resort for a while."

Charlotte nodded.

"Lissie and JT contacted a wildlife rescue group right after the helicopters landed. The rescue team will pick up the wolf pups tomorrow," Mr. Ramsey informed her.

Charlotte breathed a sigh of relief. "Oh, good! I've been thinking about those poor little guys. And what about JT?"

"He's going to stay in one of the staff bunkhouses here on the ranch for a few months. Lissie talked to her boss and arranged it so that JT can help out on the ranch in exchange for his room and board," Mr. Ramsey explained. "It'll give him time to decide what he wants to do in the long run."

"Lissie's grandmother, Amaryllis, and JT have talked by phone a few times, haven't they?" Charlotte asked.

Mr. Ramsey nodded. "I think they're both a little taken aback by the turn of events. But also very happy."

Charlotte couldn't help but smile. What a reunion it must have been! "Do you happen to know what they said to each other? Maeve was begging for me to find out EVERY detail," Charlotte told her dad.

Mr. Ramsey put his arm around Charlotte. "All I know is that they've been talking about the past and the future, and it seems they're enjoying talking after all these years. I think you detectives have done enough snooping into JT's life. It's best to let him be now."

Charlotte knew her dad was right. Still, she wished she could have been a fly on the wall during one of the conversations between JT and his long-lost Amaryllis.

Mr. Ramsey inched the door to the suite open, assuming that all the girls had crashed for the evening, but the light was on and they were all watching TV on the huge leather couch.

"Can't sleep?" Mr. Ramsey asked.

"Nope," Katani answered. "This has been a whirlwind few days. We need some time to chill!"

"Have fun," Mr. Ramsey said, "but don't stay up too late." He retired into the master bedroom, leaving the girls to catch up.

"This has been one crazy trip," Isabel said. "We missed you guys so much!"

"We missed you, too," Maeve said. "I can't believe how much has happened in the past few days. How are we ever going to go back to our normal lives? Someone should totally make a TV movie about us."

"Well, I think I'm at least going to write an article about it for the *Sentinel*," Charlotte told them, pulling her diary from her backpack. "I have plenty of notes to work from. Maybe someday I'll even write a short story about Amaryllis and JT. I'll have to change their names, of course."

"Dry Gulch was awesome! Someone should make that place a museum or something," Avery said. "Hey, Char, maybe you could get your article published in some Montana newspapers too. It might get people interested in preserving Dry Gulch so people could visit it without having to sleep on the floor and eat beans three times a day."

"Bannack became a Montana State Park!" Charlotte exclaimed. "Why couldn't something like that happen to Dry Gulch?"

"Yeah! Why not? Especially with an *original* Dry Gulch resident still alive. Maybe JT could run ghost tours or something!" Avery suggested.

"Maybe," Charlotte said thoughtfully. "But I'm not sure JT will want to be involved if it gets to be really big. He kind of likes to keep to himself, remember?"

"I guess." Avery shrugged.

"So . . ." Maeve said to Katani and Isabel. "You have to tell me every single thing you learned about Nik and Sam this week."

"Well, we were really worried about you. But once we heard the message from Mr. Ramsey that you were okay, we were able to relax a little. And have some fun with our new friends!" Katani grinned.

"Life in Montana is totally different from Boston or Detroit," Isabel surmised. "I like this place. It's very relaxed, and everyone is so friendly."

"But a little wild, too," Avery added. "Yee HAW!"

"Come on! Nik and Sam?!" Maeve demanded. "Did you get celebrity treatment all week? I am so jealous. I can't stand it!"

"Katani and I were talking about it this morning. We were really surprised at how Nik and Sam are just like regular girls," said Isabel.

"What do you mean?" Maeve asked.

Isabel tried to explain. "When I first met them, I was thinking it'd be all about the celebrity treatment too. But Nik and Sam just wanted to hang out and do normal stuff."

"Yeah," Katani agreed. "The twins love to sing, but they seemed to have just as much fun singing in the car as they did at the concert."

"That means they're *classy* celebrities. That's the kind of star I'm going to be," Maeve promised. "I'll never forget my true friends."

"My grandmother was right," Katani decided. "Seeing different places is good research. I can't wait to work some western style into my new designs. But chilling out with my best friends is so much more important right now," Katani admitted.

"This has been the best week!" Charlotte enthused.

Maeve let out a giggle that turned into a hiccup.

"You giccupped!" Avery cried. "Awesome."

"What's so funny anyway?" Katani asked.

"I was thinking about supersleek Kgirl meets laid back 'Home on the Range' style. It's a brand new concept." Maeve giggled again.

The other girls started humming "Home on the Range" as Maeve continued. "So, are you going to spring for a new pair of boots to go along with your cowgirl attitude?"

"Hmmm." Katani thought for a moment.

"Maybe a pair of pink boots? We could match!" Maeve clapped her hands together.

"No way!" Katani shook her head.

"But I thought you broadened your fashion horizons!" Maeve teased.

"Not as far as matching pink boots! And anyway, I just decided. I'm going to buy bright red ones. For Kelley."

The girls all nodded in approval.

"Kelley will love red cowboy boots!" Maeve exclaimed.

"So what about you, Maeve?" Charlotte asked. "What did you learn in the last few days?"

"Well, I can't say I'm convinced there aren't ghosts out there somewhere. And I'm so glad to be sleeping in a real cozy bed tonight. I NEVER want to eat a can of beans for breakfast again. But mostly I'm happy because I got to see a real, live storybook romance unfold before my very eyes," Maeve sighed. "Imagine thinking you were all alone in the world and then finding a grand-daughter . . . and discovering that your long-lost love is still alive after all."

Charlotte looked around the room and realized what she'd learned during the trip. That no matter what—even if he got a real girlfriend someday—her dad loved her to pieces, and that she'd never be alone in the world with her four amazing friends by her side.

To be continued . . .

Ghost Town

BOOK EXTRAS

Book Club Buzz

Trivialicious Trivia

Charlotte's Word Nerd Dictionary

Montana-Rama

The Big Bad Truth

Book Club Buzz

10 Questions for You and Your Friends to Chat About

1. Mr. Ramsey gives the BSG the chance to take a trip of a lifetime to a cool resort in the Wild Wild West. What's your dream vacation destination? What sorts of things would you want to see and do there?

2. Maeve and Isabel have to work extra hard to earn money for the trip to Big Sky Resort. Have you ever worked to earn money for something special? What did you do to earn the money? How did you spend it?

3. Why does JT stay in Dry Gulch after all those lonely years? Do you think he's happy living a solitary life? Why or why not?

4. Charlotte finds a secret diary that holds an important key to a long lost romance.

Do you keep a diary? If so, why is it important to you? What kinds of things do you write in it? How would you feel if someone else found it and read it?

5. How do Charlotte, Avery, and Maeve work together to solve the mystery of Dry Gulch?

6. Do you think Lissie and Charlotte could become friends? Why was Charlotte so nervous about Lissie at first?

7. Katani is excited about riding horses at Big Sky, but when she gets to the ranch she finds another sport she's good at. What are your unique talents? Have you ever discovered you have a talent for something that you didn't think you could do at first?

8. The group stranded in Dry Gulch has to make do with limited supplies. If you were stranded somewhere, what are the top three things you'd want to have with you?

9. Charlotte, Avery, and Maeve have a totally different experience in Montana than Katani and Isabel. Who do you think got the better end of the deal? Would you rather visit a posh resort or a cool, historic ghost town?

10. The BSG are surprised that country stars
    Nik and Sam are just like them—real girls
    with real feelings who like to hang out
    with their friends and do "normal" stuff.
    Were you surprised at how down-to-earth
    Nik and Sam are? What would you say or do
    if you met a celebrity?

Ghost Town trivialicious trivia

1. What is the name of the resort in Montana where the BSG and Mr. Ramsey are headed for the trip of a lifetime?
    A. Wolfpup Ranch
    B. Montana Dude Ranch
    C. Big Sky Resort
    D. Lissie MacMillan Resort

2. Who has the most questions for Mr. Ramsey about the trip to Montana?
    A. Mrs. Fields
    B. Aunt Lourdes
    C. Charlotte
    D. Ms. Rodriguez

3. Who calms Maeve down when she is freaking out on the plane?
    A. Nik and Sam
    B. Riley Lee
    C. Lissie
    D. Aaron Olcrest

4. What type of music do Nik and Sam sing?
    A. Jazz
    B. Country
    C. Hip-Hop
    D. Classical

5. What is the name of the ghost town where some of the BSG get stuck?
    A. Dry Gulch
    B. Green Springs
    C. Millertown
    D. Grand View

6. What kind of animals has JT been rescuing on the sly?
   A. Blue jays
   B. Wolf pups
   C. Miniature horses
   D. Bears

7. What ingredient does Maeve use to make a new and improved kind of s'more?
   A. Peanut butter
   B. M&Ms
   C. Swedish Fish
   D. Sardines

8. What sport does Katani discover she is a "natural" at?
   A. Soccer
   B. Table tennis
   C. Dogsledding
   D. Pool

9. What color are the scarves Katani gives to Nik and Sam?
   A. Navy blue and white
   B. Lime green and purple
   C. Purple and red
   D. Light blue and yellow

10. What do the initials "J.T." stand for?
    A. Jericho Tanner
    B. Jamie Talbot
    C. Jessica Tildsley
    D. Jasper Tucker

Charlotte Ramsey

Charlotte's Word Nerd Dictionary

Mammoth: (p. 1) adjective—*huge; gigantic; enormous*

Sufficient: (p. 7) adjective—*enough; the right amount*

Amenities: (p. 12) noun—*special features and offerings*

Profit: (p. 15) noun—*the money you walk away with after subtracting any expenses*

Chandelier: (p. 29) noun—*a fancy ceiling light*

Surge: (p. 33) noun—*a big rush or burst of movement*

Exasperated: (p. 46) adjective—*annoyed or irritated*

Ominous: (p. 65) adjective—*threatening; spelling disaster*

Concierge: (p. 71) noun—*employee at a resort who makes sure all the guests are comfortable*

Giddy: (p. 72) adjective—*super duper excited*

Plush: (p. 72) adjective—*cushy, luxurious, and oh-so-comfortable*

Bravado: (p. 83) noun—*a whole lot of bravery and courage*

Catapult: (p. 98) verb—*to be thrown forward*

Silhouette: (p. 112) noun—*a shadowy outline of a person or thing*

Delicacy: (p. 116) noun—*a truly special, unique, and often expensive type of food*

Equestrian: (p. 135) adjective—*relating to horses*

Pungent: (p. 145) adjective—*strong smelling or tasting*

Memento: (p. 162) noun—*something special that reminds you of something that happened in the past*

Peruse: (p. 174) verb—*to read something very carefully*

Definitions adapted from *Webster's Dictionary*,
Fourth Edition, Random House.

Montana-Rama!

Big Fun Facts about Big Sky Country

What do you mean there's a Spanish Mountain next to Idaho?
The name "Montana" comes from the Spanish word for mountain: "montaña."

Move over, Nessie!

Flathead Lake, seven miles south of Kalispell, Montana, is said to be home to the legendary Flathead Lake Monster. The first reported sighting of this large, underwater animal was in the late 1880s. Since then, many people think they've glimpsed the colossal creature, but no one has yet identified it. Is it a sea monster? A dinosaur? Or just a really big fish? YOU decide!

Reserve a space for me!
Montana is home to seven Native American reservations: Blackfeet, Crow Creek, Flathead, Fort Belknap, Fort Peck, Northern Cheyenne, and Rocky Boy's. Every August, Montana residents celebrate the state's Native American heritage at

the Crow Fair and Rodeo, a festival featuring parades, horse races, and traditional costumes and dancing.

Let it snow . . .
The largest snowflake ever recorded was found at Fort Keogh, Montana, in 1887. Unbelievably, this fabulous flake measured eight inches thick and nearly fifteen inches across. With snowflakes like that, no wonder Montana is called "Big Sky Country!"

Huckleberry Haven
Trout Creek, Montana, is home to the Huckleberry Festival, started almost thirty years ago. People from all over the world attend to taste and buy these berries, which are indigenous to the Pacific Northwest. The Festival features huckleberry ice cream, huckleberry pizza, huckleberry cheesecake . . . and who could forget the Miss Huckleberry Pageant?

Dino-mite!
Buried beneath Montana's breathtaking canyons and mountain ranges are tons (literally!) of fossilized dinosaur bones. In fact, Montana is an especially good place to look for the bones of duckbilled dinosaurs, or hadrosaurs. And these fossils really "rock": the first hadrosaur unearthed in Montana was nicknamed "Elvis"!

The Big Bad Truth

An Avery Madden Crazy Critters Exclusive

After hearing all those fairytales my mom read to me as a kid, I thought I had the scoop on wolves: BIG and BAD. I mean, just ask the three little pigs if you need the proof! But that *bad* reputation isn't entirely true, says William T. Wolf, a long-time resident of Montana who also just so happens to be a member of this noble species. Since these furry gray guys usually get such a bad rap, I decided to give him a shot at setting the record straight—as long as there's no howling involved!

Avery Madden: So which are you, Will, big or bad?

William T. Wolf: Well, if you put it that way, I guess I'll go with big. Around my parts—that's western Montana, mostly—we're members of the species *canis lupus*, although you can just call me a gray wolf. And since you're so stuck on this size issue, I'll have you know that I'm about five and a half feet long, from the tip of my nose to the end of my tail.

AM: Whoa, you're bigger than me!

WW: But what I'm tryin' to tell ya, Avery, is that we might be *big*, but we're not all *bad*. In fact, from our point of view, you humans seem pretty scary!

AM: Really? Puny little us?

WW: Well sure. Back around sixty-five years ago, you guys pretty much drove my family out of its home. Thanks to human hunting, by 1940 there were no gray wolves in Montana anymore.

AM: Wow, I never thought of it that way. I guess who's "bad" all depends on how you look at it. So one last question: if you're not really bad, then what are all those *forty-two* gleaming white teeth for?

WW: The better to talk with you, my dear.

Share the Next

BEACON STREET GIRLS

Adventure

Time's Up

Katani knows she can win the business contest. But with school and friends and family taking up all her time, has she gotten in over her head?

Check out the Beacon Street Girls at

beaconstreetgirls.com

Aladdin M!X

Here's an excerpt from the

next adventure,
Time's Up

They have harnesses and stuff, right?" Maeve asked in a tremulous voice. "I mean, to catch you if you fall off?" At the words "fall off," Katani swallowed hard. She too felt nervous at the sight of the ginormous, gray climbing wall. *I can't believe I'm actually going to climb it,* she thought. But she reached down and gave Maeve's clammy hand a reassuring squeeze. "Chillax, girlfriend. Look at Avery. She can't fall." Sure enough, Avery, the most athletic of the group of friends, was already securely harnessed and had started her climb.

Katani tried to distract herself from her fears of looking like a total spaz on the wall by concentrating on her favorite magazine, *T-Biz! A Magazine for Teen Entrepreneurs.* As she flipped another page with her free hand, a colorful ad suddenly caught her eye. "This is incredible!" she blurted out loud, before she could stop herself.

"Whoa! That's the spirit, Katani!" Avery shouted encouragingly, giving the Kgirl a thumbs-up as she dangled in her harness.

Katani looked up, slightly embarrassed by her outburst but glowing with excitement about what she had read. "No, no, it's not that, Ave. Forget the wall. It's this contest—an 'Entrepreneur of the Year' contest for middle-school students! Listen . . ." But Avery was already facing the wall and the pint-size climber hadn't heard a word she had said. Katani figured Avery was probably too busy trying to beat the boy next to her up the wall.

"You better put that magazine away, Miss Fashion Biz, and listen to the instructor, or you'll be hanging every which way when it's your turn," warned a suddenly serious Maeve, her big blue eyes glued to the climbers scrambling up the wall like little spider people. Maeve gasped as one climber slipped and fell away from the wall.

But Katani couldn't care less about the rock climbers. In fact, she wished she had stayed home. *T-Biz!* was seeking "the next generation of business leaders." This was *so* up her alley. Kgirl Enterprises was her ultimate fantasy. She should be home now writing up her "detailed, viable business plan" instead of climbing like a giant bug up some *craaazy* wall. Why had she agreed to come? The contest offered "an opportunity for all young entrepreneurs to fulfill their dreams." Katani looked around to see if she could find a quiet place to keep reading.

A sudden blur on the rock wall grabbed her attention. "That girl just fell ten feet!" she yelped.

Maeve, who had been waving for Charlotte and Isabel

to come over, spun around. The little girl was now hanging in midair. Maeve's legs began to tremble.

"She's fine," a boy standing behind the girls said.

Maeve turned around to see two of their friends from school. "Hey! Dillon and Nick! What are you doing here?"

"How can Isabel just stand over there and draw?" Katani commented, glancing over at Isabel, who was intently sketching one of the climbers. "My hands are shaking so much, I don't think I could hold a pencil!" she said as she quickly zipped her magazine in the pocket of her sweatshirt. While she liked Dillon and Nick, no way was she ready to share that she was going to enter the *T-Biz!* entrepreneur contest with the two most popular boys at Abigail Adams Junior High. Dillon could be a big tease, and she didn't want to be his latest target. She could just hear him in the cafeteria announcing, "Katani's going to be on the next *Oprah*. Uh-huh!"

Collect all the BSG books today!

#1 Worst Enemies/Best Friends ☐ **READ IT!**
Yikes! As if being the new girl isn't bad enough . . . Charlotte just made the
biggest cafeteria blunder in the history of Abigail Adams Junior High.

#2 Bad News/Good News ☐ **READ IT!**
Charlotte can't believe it. Her father wants to move away again, and the
timing couldn't be worse for the Beacon Street Girls.

#3 Letters from the Heart ☐ **READ IT!**
Life seems perfect for Maeve and Avery . . . until they find out that in
seventh grade, the world can turn upside down just like that.

#4 Out of Bounds ☐ **READ IT!**
Can the Beacon Street Girls bring the house down at Abigail Adams Junior
High's Talent Show? Or will the Queens of Mean steal the show?

#5 Promises, Promises ☐ **READ IT!**
Tensions rise when two BSG find themselves in a tight race for seventh-
grade president at Abigail Adams Junior High.

#6 Lake Rescue ☐ **READ IT!**
The seventh grade outdoor trip promises lots o' fun for the BSG—but will the
adventure prove too much for one sensitive classmate?

#7 Freaked Out ☐ **READ IT!**
The party of the year is just around the corner. What happens when the
party invitations are given out . . . but not to everyone?

#8 Lucky Charm ☐ **READ IT!**
Marty is missing! The BSG's frantic search for their beloved pup leads them to
a very famous person and the game of a lifetime.

#9 Fashion Frenzy ☐ **READ IT!**
Katani and Maeve are off to the Big Apple for a supercool teen fashion
show. Will tempers fray in close quarters?

#10 Just Kidding ☐ **READ IT!**
The BSG are looking forward to Spirit Week at Abigail Adams Junior High, until
some mean—and untrue—gossip about Isabel dampens everyone's spirits.

#11 Ghost Town
The BSG's fun-filled week at a Montana dude ranch includes skiing, snow-boarding, cowboys, and celebrity twins—plus a ghost town full of secrets.

#12 Time's Up
Katani knows she can win the business contest. But with school and friends and family taking up all her time, has she gotten in over her head?

#13 Green Algae and Bubble Gum Wars
Inspired by the Sally Ride Science Fair, the BSG go green, but getting stuck slimed by some gooey supergum proves to be a major annoyance!

#14 Crush Alert
Romantic triangles and confusion abound as the BSG look forward to the Abigail Adams Junior High Valentine's Day dance.

#15 The Great Scavenger Hunt
Winning an ocean-side scavenger hunt isn't nearly as exciting for some of the BSG as surfing and beach volleyball or the chance to fulfill a Hollywood dream—with pirates!

Also . . . Our Special Adventure Series:

Charlotte in Paris
Something mysterious happens when Charlotte returns to Paris to search for her long-lost cat and to visit her best Parisian friend, Sophie.

Maeve on the Red Carpet
A cool film camp at the Movie House is a chance for Maeve to become a star, but newfound fame has a downside for the perky redhead.

Freestyle with Avery
Avery Madden can't wait to go to Telluride, Colorado, to visit her dad! But there's one surprise that Avery's definitely not expecting.

Katani's Jamaican Holiday
A lost necklace and a plot to sabotage her family's business threaten to turn Katani's dream beach vacation in Jamaica into stormy weather.

Isabel's Texas Two-Step
A disastrous accident with a valuable work of art and a sister with a diva attitude give Isabel a bad case of the ups and downs on a special family trip.

FREE Club for you and your BFFs on BeaconStreetGirls.com!

If you loved this book, you'll love hanging out with the **Beacon Street Girls** (BSG)! **Join the BSG** (and their dog Marty) for virtual sleepovers, fashion tips, celeb interviews, games and more!

And with **Marty's secret code** (below), start getting **totally free stuff right away!**

MARTY'$MONEY™
VIRTUAL RESERVE NOTE

CLUB

BSG

SECRET CODE
GHT298113

MARTY

FIVE DOLLARS

BEACONSTREETGIRLS.COM

BEACON STREET GIRLS

MARTY'$MONEY is **not** legal tender. **MARTY'$MONEY** can only be used on **www.BeaconStreetGirls.com** to purchase virtual gifts online for your Club BSG friends and **cannot** be used to purchase 'real world' gifts at the BSGshop.

To get **$5** in **MARTY'$MONEY** (one per person) go to **www.BeaconStreetGirls.com/redeem** and follow the instructions, while supplies last.

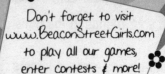